Shout of Honor
Adventures in the Liaden Universe® Number 29

Sharon Lee and Steve Miller

COPYRIGHT PAGE

Shout of Honor: Adventures in the Liaden Universe® Number 29

Pinbeam Books: www.pinbeambooks.com

This is a work of fiction. All the characters and events portrayed in this novel are fiction or are used fictitiously.

"Shout of Honor" is original to this chapbook

Cover Design: SelfPubBookCovers.com/RLSather
ISBN: 978-1-948465-05-2

DEDICATION

To the Librarians of Earth, who bring connections out of chaos,
and learning to those who seek it

THANK YOU

Barbara Karpel and Anne Young for their eagle eyes and expertise

CHAPTER ONE

They came into Inago for news, and supplies, and other such items of interest that a way station might be expected to offer. Vepal had chosen this particular way station because it was in a more populated sector and enjoyed a level of traffic that the ports they usually chose did not.

Traffic, then, he had expected.

He had simply not expected *so much* traffic.

Nor that so much of it would be . . .martial . . .in nature.

Some might have leapt to the conclusion that Inago was under attack. Commander Vepal's trained eye immediately discerned the lack of lines, the lack of order in committed approaches. Oh, there was *station* order, this ship to *such* berth on *that* heading–but nothing like military discipline, or thinking, here.

But if not an attack, then–what brought so many soldiers and fighting ships to Inago Prime, surely among the least warlike location in this section of space?

His board pinged receipt of a communication originating at the station. Not, according to the wrapper, from station admin–they were too far out, yet, for the station master's attention. No, this message originated inside the station; sent from a private source.

Intrigued, Vepal opened the packet.

Perdition Enterprises is hiring soldiers, pilots, techs, and specialists for assignments starting immediately! All may apply–papers or paper-free; lone guns to entire units. Soldiers and specialists must have own kit. Working units will be retained intact, if possible. All contracts with Perdition Enterprises. PE provides transportation, target, mis-

3

*sion goals, and timeline. Generous bonuses for early completion! NDA
required. Come to Core Conference, station center, any hour, any day.
Recruiters standing by.*

The message began to repeat, and Vepal killed it.

"Are we looking for employment?" Pilot Erthax asked, and
waited just a breath too long before adding, "Sir."

Vepal considered him.

"I've been going over the mission's funding. Temp Headquarters used to omit only one of our five stipends per Cycle. Of the last
five due, we have received . . .three.

"This lack of funding decreases our efficiency and our scope,"
Vepal went on, talking quietly, gaze on his screen. "It might be . . .to
the benefit of the mission to find what this Perdition Enterprises
considers reasonable recompense for the skills of a pilot. If there is
a signing bonus, as well . . ."

Though he kept his eyes scrupulously on his screen, Vepal's peripheral vision was good enough that he saw Erthax's hard, dark
face flush, and his mouth tighten.

"Yes," he continued. "You make a good point, Pilot. We should
definitely find what assignments are on offer, and of what duration.
It seems to me that we have become soft in our small unit here. A
stint in the field might be what is required."

He was. . .not joking. Jokes were made between comrades. No,
he was deliberately egging Erthax on, out of temper and dislike.

Which, he thought, with some chagrin, proved his point. They
had become soft of discipline. *He* had become soft, for it was true
that the troop was the reflection of command. And a commander
who would taunt one of his own soldiers . . .ought to offer himself
to the High Command for a field tour at reduced rank.

Which, interestingly enough, was what Perdition Enterprises offered.

Vepal frowned at his screen. It was outside of his authority to enlist in a military action, even if Perdition Enterprises included Yxtrang among those it found acceptable. Papers or paper-free, was it? Legitimate, licensed soldiers fighting beside pirates, renegades–and Yxtrang?

Still, there was opportunity here. The point of his mission was to discover, per the continuing orders from Headquarters, the proper entity for those of the Troop who had survived the collapse of the old universe to offer their allegiance, and their skills.

It seemed. . .unlikely that Perdition Enterprises was that entity, but it was not. . .*entirely* unlikely that they might have information about such an entity.

For almost the first time since he had re-discovered their continuing orders, lost for hundreds of Cycles, Vepal felt a stirring of hope, that this was not entirely the mission of a fool.

#

The answer to his request for an interview with a recruiter upon their arrival on Inago, was–an application.

A form letter asked that he complete the application and send it ahead so that an appointment with an appropriate recruiter could be made. There was also a brief and uninformative blurb, from which he learned that Perdition Enterprises was in the business of brokering military and quasi-military assignments. There was no information about those in command, the owners or directors. The planet upon which Perdition Enterprises was registered was–not Waymart. Not quite Waymart.

It was, however, registered, licensed, and approved by the Better Business Bureau of Gilstommer, which, as Vepal understood it, was to corporate entities precisely what Waymart was to ships.

So, the application.

He applied as "Vepal Small Troop," listing their personnel as one senior officer with advanced piloting and command skills, one line pilot, and one line soldier, detailing the skills shared among the troop, save those specific to Explorers. In a section headed "Other Assets," he noted that the troop maintained its own vessel, lightly armed and armored, suitable for reconnaissance or courier. He admitted that their treasury was small, and added that each member carried a complete and well-maintained kit.

Put thus, they looked a sad case, indeed, and he hesitated overlong, wondering if he ought to expand their worth. It was his purpose to gain an interview to learn about these *immediate assignments*, and to put particular questions of his own.

In the end, however, he sent in the nearly-truthful application.

And, to his very great surprise, a communication from Perdition Enterprises met them at the dock, naming an hour not too far distant for Commander Vepal to meet with Recruiter pen'Chouka, in the Core Conference Center, Room 9A.

Vepal considered the name, which suggested that the recruiting agent was . . .Liaden. It was well to consider beforehand, how a Liaden might react, confronted with an Yxtrang, even a certified and guaranteed safe Yxtrang.

Still—Perdition Enterprises encouraged all to apply—papers or paper-free, eh? Surely Recruiting Agent pen'Chouka had seen worse than a well-behaved Yxtrang commander, respectfully reporting for his interview in dress uniform, with only small arm and grace blade on the belt; his honor-marks old and faded, and grey showing in his hair.

He had been instructed to appear unaccompanied before Recruiting Agent pen'Chouka, which Ochin would not like. The central belief of the Rifle's life was that Commander Vepal ought always to be accompanied by an escort appropriate to his rank–an honor guard at least!–or by the escort available, which would be Ochin Rifle.

Vepal hesitated. He didn't like to disappoint his Rifle, who was a simple man, and loyal, as Erthax was not. Still, the request was not unreasonable; was, in fact, prudent, and efficient. Evaluate command first, as the face and mind of the troop. If the commander passed inspection, then he would be called back, with his troop, for a second evaluation, if the first interview proved not to be sufficient.

On the way in to the station, he had attempted further research on Perdition Enterprises, but beyond the information contained in the brief blurb provided by the company itself, and a great deal of chatter on the social nets regarding a large hire-on at Inago, with guaranteed good pay, he found nothing.

It was somewhat worrisome that there was nothing in the chatter from those who had *been* hired; maybe the non-disclosure agreement prevented such. Again, that would be . . .not unreasonable.

And the only way to discover anything more substantial, apparently, was to attend Recruiting Agent pen'Chouka. Commander Vepal glanced at the time display, and at the route to Room 9A in the Core Conference Area outlined on his screen.

Time to leave.

He inspected himself once more in the mirror, seeing that everything was soldierly. Satisfied, he picked up his hat and left their dock, stopping first to issue specific orders to Erthax and Ochin, and to state the time by which he ought to have returned, or contacted the ship with an amended hour of arrival.

#

"Commander Vepal, welcome."

Recruiting Agent pen'Chouka was, indeed, Liaden, dressed in what might be the off-duty uniform of a common Troop–leather vest over a close-necked shirt, with long, tight sleeves. Nothing to snag, nothing to flutter, nothing to call attention. As the recruiter rose to meet him, Vepal was also able to see the small arm on the right side of his belt, and the dagger on the left, before the day-pouch.

"Recruiting Agent, I thank you," Vepal said, wondering if the man would dare a proper salute.

He did not. Merely, he inclined very slightly from the waist, and on straightening, moved a hand to show Vepal the other person, similarly dressed, who had also risen.

"My associate, Agent ter'Menth, who has been asked to sit in on this interview."

It was not said who had made this request; quite possibly a senior officer, if Perdition Enterprises was, in fact, modeled on military organization. Certainly, had their places been reversed, Vepal would have produced at the least a soft show of strength for a soldier of an enemy race.

"Please," said Recruiting Agent pen'Chouka, "let us sit and discuss the matter before us. Commander, may I offer you refreshment?"

The room was small and bare, holding the recruiting agent's desk, with a large screen set to one side, angled so that he might see the information displayed there, but the applicant could not. A portable data pad sat near the recruiter's right hand—and that was all and everything, save the chairs they sat on—inside the boundaries of the room.

Refreshment would therefore need to be called in, adding to the time it would take him to find out what Perdition Enterprises was recruiting for, and also introducing the risk that the refreshment would be . . .impure.

"Thank you," he said, which even a Liaden would recognize as politely civilized, "but no."

"Certainly," said Recruiter pen'Chouka, equitably, "let us immediately to business."

He glanced at the large screen.

"May I say, we were gratified to receive your application, Commander? Of course we will have room for such a *small troop* as you propose. We anticipate no difficulties."

Vepal trusted that his face remained soldierly. They had him travel half-way across the station to a private meeting only to accept his troop's application without discussion? A chill swept down his spine, not unlike the sensation he had when he sensed an ambush.

"I hadn't realized that our troop was so well-known among the wide field of fighters," he said carefully, watching the recruiter's face, which, Liaden-wise, told him nothing.

"Oh," he said, with what might have been a small smile at the corner of the mouth, "your reputation proceeds you, sir; I assure you."

"In that case," Vepal said, still treading carefully, "you will know that I cannot commit without having some information regarding the scope of the mission. Our group has other obligations . . ."

"Of course it does," said the recruiter soothingly. He picked up the data pad and offered it to Vepal.

"You will have all of the information you require, Commander. Simply sign the non-disclosure agreement, and–"

Vepal did not extend a hand to receive the screen. Instead, he directed a piercing glance at the recruiter's face, lips parted, and allowing a little tooth to be seen, while he considered the implications of non-disclosure agreements. He knew of such things, but it had been his impression that they were brought into the negotiations after a certain level of basic trust had been established. To offer the thing up to be signed immediately, before any attempt at trust-building . . .

"Some basic information would be welcome," he said, austerely. "I cannot commit resources simply because Perdition Enterprises finds our reputation admirable."

Recruiting Agent pen'Chouka placed the pad on the table by Vepal's folded hands, and inclined his head.

"Basic information–of course! Perdition Enterprises is a combat broker. In short, we bring grievances together with forces appropriate to resolving them. I will tell you, Commander Vepal, that we are presently recruiting for a large-scale event; very complex. I believe that you, as others before you, will find our compensation package to be very good, and the bonus structure generous. I hardly need say that, for such a troop as yours, there is room for negotiation."

"What is the projected duration of this event?" he asked, but Recruiting Agent pen'Chouka held up his hands, showing empty palms.

"Sign the agreement, Commander, and all the information I have is yours."

Vepal sat very still, considering his options.

"Commander, may I ask a question?" The other recruiter–ter'Menth–spoke for the first time; her voice light, and her Terran bearing not the slightest accent.

He looked to her, keeping her partner in peripheral vision.

"You may ask," he said, watching her eyes.

This one was a killer, he thought. Doubtless the other was, too, but this one made no effort to hide herself behind affable politeness, as if Vepal were Terran; easily soothed by smiles and soft words.

Recruiting Agent ter'Menth inclined her head.

"I thank you. I wonder–indeed, we had *all* wondered, immediately we saw your application, and your docking packet–is it possible that you speak for. . .a force larger than the small troop which travels with you? Perdition is prepared to be generous, even beyond our A-level contract, if you have a proposal in mind. You are, in fact, the answer to a conundrum we had not hoped to solve."

"I do not understand you," Vepal said, which was not entirely untruthful. "Please speak plainly, Recruiter."

She smiled, showing the teeth, as might a soldier who wished to establish precedence.

"Since you ask so gently," she began, and stopped in order to look at her partner, who had made a small noise, perhaps of denial.

"I take full responsibility," she said, and after a long moment, he bowed his head.

She turned back to Vepal.

"I will be plain," she said. "The scope of the project before us is such that we thought of contacting Yxtrang Command with an offer. We found no clear way to do so, and those sent to intercept your ambassadorial team failed, so far as we know, to arrive. Thus, we turned to our secondary plan, with reluctance. However, now that *you* have brought the ambassadorial team to *us*, perhaps you might assist us in approaching the High Command at . . .at Temp Headquarters with an offer."

He stared at her, and suddenly there was nothing more that he wanted from his life than to leave this room, alive.

"I may be able to assist," he said, slowly. "But in order to do so, I will need to know the details of your offer. I will tell you that the High Commanders are . . .unlikely to sign a non-disclosure agreement."

She smiled again, seeming genuinely amused.

"Of course we do not intend to deal with the High Command as we treat with mere mercenary soldiers and bully squads. What we propose is to offer the High Command a contract."

"A–*contract*," he repeated, the word sounding ominous in his head. "For what purpose?"

She leaned forward, her elbows on the table, and gazed up into his face.

"We wish to contract the services of a full Conquest Corps to destroy a target of our choosing."

CHAPTER TWO

He had escaped, with his life, and a very small additional amount of information. Recruiting Agent ter'Menth had not bothered to pretend that what she gave him was in any way useful. On his side, he pretended that what she offered was something that the High Commanders might wish to consider.

What he did not say was that the High Commanders would not accept a contract. The Troop were not *soldiers for hire*; they were *the Troop*. Created to take the war to an unbeatable enemy. Created to stand rear guard so that the civilians the Troop, from its position of bred superiority, protected, might escape with their lives, and find safety . . .elsewhere.

Sadly, his innate superiority had not been sufficient to disentangle him completely from Perdition Enterprises. Recruiting Agent ter'Menth expected an answer. She expected, in fact, that he would return to his ship and forthwith send a courier-beam to High Command, laying before them the wonders of this contract, which included rich looting, and the opportunity for more, like, contracts.

He was–not quite–so foolish as to do anything like. But what he must do, and quickly, was to leave this port, with his small troop intact.

Despite that goal burning brightly in his mind, he did not immediately return to dock, ship, and troop. He was in no fit condition to return to his command. Even Ochin would see that there was something amiss. He needed time to settle himself, to make a plan for removing them safely from the reach of Perdition Enterprises.

So, he called the ship, amended his arrival time, and was now seated at a back table at an eating and drinking establishment called, according to the sign over the door, *The Headless Yxtrang*. It could hardly be more fitting. He ordered beer and a soy-cheese handwich. He wanted neither, but the order would secure the table for an hour.

And give him a chance to think.

The existence of the Yxtrang Ambassador to the Outworlds was known among a certain set of persons with a need to know—the Liaden Scouts, the Portmasters Guild, the Pilots Guild.

Perdition Enterprises, being a broker of war, would naturally make it their business to likewise know such things.

A team had been sent to him, but never arrived, so ter'Menth had said. Was that a fact? If so, what had happened to that team? Had it defected? Been captured? Been diverted to another assignment?

Had—

"Ambassador Vepal," a clear, memorable voice said, carrying inflections of both surprise and—pleasure? "You may remember me, sir, from Seebrit Station."

He raised his head to meet black eyes set in a strong, lean face.

"Commander Sanchez."

He stood, out of respect for her rank, and for the scar that adorned her right cheek. Many have known the caress of the war blade, though few survive it. That JinJee Sanchez was one of those few—pleased him in a way that he could not have explained. She was a warrior, and intelligent; an equal, which he had in neither Ochin nor Erthax.

"I remember you, Commander, and I am pleased to see you well."

There, that was polite and civilized.

Sanchez smiled like to the smile that passed between old comrades, chance-met off the field.

"I am glad to see you well–and to see you again. May I join you?"

Join him? Ah, she meant to sit at his table, and share time over the meal.

"I would welcome your presence," he told her truthfully.

She sat across from him, her shoulder to the room, while he resumed the seat that gave him the wider view. Among comrades, this would indicate that he was point in this place and time. It was gratifying, that she allowed him this honor.

Gratifying–and strangely troubling.

"I will have what this, my comrade, is having," Sanchez was telling the waiter. "All to go onto the Paladins account."

He blinked, was about to protest that he was able to feed himself–and subsided at the bare shake of her head.

"Allow me to discharge the remainder of my debt to your good nature," she said, gravely.

"If you feel such a debt exists," he told her; "I do not."

"Another display of good-nature!" she said, with a certain lightness to her voice.

Her handwich and beer appeared on the table before her. She nodded without taking her eyes from Vepal's face.

"I wonder to find you here," she said. "Did you come for the job fair?"

"I came to find information to assist me in my duty," he told her. "The . . .job fair was a surprise."

"Ah." She picked up her beer and had a swallow. "Then you have not been to the recruiting office."

"I've just come from the recruiting office," he said, following her lead. The beer was good, he noted with surprise.

"I went yesterday," she said, "on behalf of the Paladins. Will you tell me your impressions?"

He hesitated and she held up a hand.

"I don't ask you to violate the NDA, of course."

"I did not sign the form," he said.

Black eyebrows rose in interest.

"Oh, you didn't . . ." she said softly.

She put her elbows on the table, and leaned closer.

"Now, I am *very* interested in whatever you choose to tell me," she said.

He considered her strong face; finding honor there. She was a warrior—yes; and a fighter.

But she was not a killer.

There were details which he could not share. But there were other matters on which, he thought, he *must* speak, comrade-to-comrade, if only to help order his own thoughts.

It crossed his mind that she might have been sent from the recruiting officers, to test him. It was possible, after all, that JinJee Sanchez had signed the non-disclosure agreement, and was thus on assignment.

He picked up the mug and swallowed beer in a leisurely manner, to give himself time to think.

Even if she was constrained by orders, he decided; there were certain matters he must share with her. To do otherwise would be to further besmirch his own tattered honor.

He put the mug back on the table, and raised his eyes to meet hers.

"I am . . .dismayed by the insistence that the non-disclosure agreement must be signed before *any* information is given out. It would seem easy enough to provide specific information regarding payments and bonuses, for instance, as an incentive to sign the agreement and learn more."

She was nodding.

"They are too careful. It makes one wonder *why*, does it not? As you say, the publication of even an *average* pay scale would speedily fix the interest of some. It might be argued that they have had poor advice in how to best go forward, but the solicitations they are sending out along the merc channels promise *competitive* and even *merc scale* recompense."

She help up one hand, hefting the her mug with the other.

"Mind you, *merc scale* is fair nonsense, as any merc can tell you. But it demonstrates a willingness to entice."

He considered her.

"Did you sign the NDA?" he asked bluntly.

"I have not," she said, and gave him a bland look. "I await my co-commander before proceeding, and had merely visited the recruiting office to ensure the Paladins a place in-queue."

She lifted her mug and drank, deeply.

"Another?" she asked, when she had put the empty on the table, she nodded at his mug, which he raised and drained likewise.

"Another –yes; though I will buy this round, so that we sit together as true comrades."

"Neither beholden to the other?" she asked.

"Yes."

She inclined her head.

"I agree."

He called for the drinks. When they arrived, he looked again to JinJee Sanchez.

"When will your co-commander arrive?" he asked.

She smiled.

"When he is needed. I hope that he will *not* be needed, if I may speak frankly between comrades."

"The Paladins have no need of employment?"

"Whenever was there a mercenary troop who did not need employment? In fact, we were on our way to a hiring hall when the advertisement for this job fair crossed our comm-lines. We thought to save ourselves some weeks of travel, with only a minor adjustment of course. And, it was not immediately obvious from the tenor of the advertisement that this was not a merc-sponsored event."

"Now that you have seen it—"

"Now that I have seen it, there is no question that the mercs do not endorse Perdition Enterprises, nor do our competitors, or our sisters."

"So, this would be a new organization, seeking to establish themselves?"

"New, they certainly are, but if they seek to establish themselves *credibly*, they have chosen an odd course."

She glanced down at her plate and picked up the handwich.

"Eat, Comrade! Who knows when we will have anything other than field rations again!"

He obeyed, admiring the neat efficiency she brought to the task.

"What is odd about their course?" he asked. "Besides a tendency toward secrecy?"

"In the normal way of things, this new enterprise would have among its founding membership some few from other, more established, organizations. They would take good care to advertise the names of these founders, so that those they seek to hire, or to bring into the new structure, will feel that it is built upon the strong shoulders and experience of known professionals."

She pointed at him with her half-eaten handwich.

"Perdition Enterprises does not advertise its founders, which ought to be its greatest strength, until they have excelled in the field for half-a-dozen missions, and proven their own merit."

"And their backers?" Vepal asked. "I searched, but it was by necessity shallow and quick..."

"No, do not expend another ounce of your energy looking for their backers!" she said earnestly. "We have searched, wide, deep, and long, as my staff researcher styles it. If there are backers, they very much wish to remain out of sight, and in this one thing, says Research Officer Aritz, who does not part with such praise lightly—they are masters."

Vepal frowned.

"No backers, no founders. It's as if they *want to* be in the shadows."

"That would seem to be their preference, but they must put themselves into the light in order to recruit the troops necessary for their mission."

"Which is also a secret."

She smiled.

"Exactly."

Silence fell then as they finished their meal.

When both were done, the plates set aside, and another round of beer ordered, Vepal looked again to his comrade.

"Despite all these things, will you commit to this mission?" he asked. "Without knowing what it is?"

He did not believe it of her, yet–this supposed co-commander, who might appear from among her troop at her word, so he was certain–what reason had she to remain here, especially when her troop sought work?

"No, I do not think that I will," she said, her eyes thoughtful. "At least, I hope it will not go that far. I am . . .squeamish of my honor, and I would prefer not to put it in peril. If there is no other way, though . . ."

Her voice trailed off, and she considered the tabletop intently.

Vepal stilled, watching her think–and seeing the moment she made her decision.

"I will tell you," she said, with a nod. "I remain here because, after I met with the recruiters to ensure the place of the Paladins in queue, I was troubled by these things you and I have just discussed. That being so, I contacted an old comrade who makes it her business to know the secrets of others, hoping that she knew all and everything about Perdition Enterprises, and would therefore put my fears to rest."

She shook her head.

"She was also stymied, and she asked me if I would assist her in gathering information, for the usual fees. I agreed."

"You wish to find out who they are?"

"That–yes. There are many mercs already tangled in this–whatever it is–they having signed the NDA and been recruited. I talked to two commanders who have done so, and I will tell you, Comrade–they are not easily frightened. But I spoke to frightened mercs. *Frightened* mercs who saw no way out of what they had done, and who would not utter one word of what they had agreed to, their pay, or their assignment.

"This made me even more curious, and increased my concern three-fold. What sort of hold does Perdition Enterprises have over its recruits? So–*that* I wish also to solve."

"But who are they building forces against?" Vepal asked. "Knowing the name of the target–"

"Yes!" she said, putting warm fingers briefly on his wrist. "Yes. The answer to that question, my friend, could not only unlock the mysteries we have discussed, but it might well make us rich!"

#

"How long?" Erthax asked. "Sir."

"We will accept the full station-week available to this docking," Vepal told him, and added, "Do you have more questions, Pilot?" in a tone that strongly suggested it would be best for Erthax's health if he failed of having any more questions for the remainder of his life.

For once, Erthax took the point.

"Sir. No, sir," he said, promptly.

He then produced a reasonably sharp salute, turned briskly on his heel and left the common room. Vepal did not sigh, but merely turned to Ochin, standing patiently by the bench where his evening meal sat untouched.

"Orders, Commander?"

"You are at liberty–eat, rest, amuse yourself. Visit the small bars, if you will, and find the temper of the station. Whatever you do, you will come to me at fifth hour, in my quarters. We will discuss schedules during our time at dock. Come prepared with a list of necessary tasks which you are qualified to perform."

There was a small pause, which one might expect, given that the orders required some initiative on the part of the Rifle.

Ochin saluted.

"Sir. Yes, sir."

Vepal returned the salute, and left the common area.

In his quarters, he sat at the theoretically shielded, private comm deck. Sanchez had agreed with his analysis, that the recruitment team would expect—would be waiting for him—to send a message. If he wished to learn more about those who thought that the Troop was for hire—if he wished, as he did, to assist Sanchez and her associate to whom all secrets, save this one, were open—there was no other course, but to send a message. Security wrap, absolutely. In fact, he thought, tapping the unit up, he might as well send two messages. It was time he knew for certain whether Firge remained in a position to aid him—or if she had, as he feared, been dispatched to Duty's Reward.

The first message, then, to the Finance Officer, citing the missing payments, and demanding that the shortfall be made up, immediately. He wrapped it in as many security codes as were available to him, and hit *send* with rather more enthusiasm than a sober message concerning an employment contract on offer might be expected to excite. The watchers at Perdition Enterprises needn't know that, of course.

The second message—not to Firge, no. If she still lived, he would not for his own life endanger her. No, the second message to the Records Officer, requesting an updated roster of High Commanders, and their seconds.

That, too, traveled in a thick security wrapping.

Vepal sat for a few minutes longer, weighing whether three messages might be seen as excessive, and to whom he might address another.

In the end, he judged the two he had sent sufficient, powered off the comm deck, and sought his bed.

CHAPTER THREE

Perdition Enterprises had spies all over the station; that hardly needed to be said. They'd probably tapped in to the station's own sensors–he would have if he was in their position, after all.

Vepal of course remained at dock, awaiting the replies to his high-security messages. He made certain that his activities were public and easy to document. He availed himself of the station database, as he had done at every port since the start of the mission, sifting for hints that might point to those peoples who were worthy to accept their knives . . .or who would have mercy sufficient to save them, who had made enemies of all this universe.

He went, variously, under escort, and his own recognizance. While the ship required maintenance, he considered it advisable to allow Ochin and Erthax generous leave time, as they were, each in their way, a boon to the mission.

Men talked freely around the Rifle, discounting him despite his stature, his modest facial decoration, and his uniform. Perhaps they assumed that he had no Trade or Terran, though he was perfectly fluent in each, at his commander's order, there being nothing much else to do during their long hunt, save polish the bright work–and study. For that matter, he also had Liaden. Anyone who traveled long among the stars was bound also to have *some* Liaden to get by. For safety.

Ochin, though, went further than that. Ochin had a small collection of *melant'i* plays, an accidental discovery at a Terran station where a some down-on-the-luck spaceman had traded them at pawn for cash or some more practical item. Erthax being nearly Liaden in his interpretation of rank, and Ochin, Rifle that he was, a

wolf deprived of his pack. At times, Ochin wished for companion-
ship and turned to the plays for society. Vepal had seen him reading plays, on occasion, between required reading of regs and of rifle
lore.

On Inago, Ochin spent some of his money on packaged sweet-
foods, others on entertainments he might also return to the ship
with–the High Command not having supplied the vessel with
much in the way of games or desserts. He spent some of his time
in the low-key places dispensing soft drinks, near-beers, and lighter
inebriants along with machine amusements, clearly as much on
shore leave as any. Sitting in dark corners was a habit of some years;
he practiced his languages by listening and recalling. Occasionally,
he'd be joined by a merc looking to be quiet and to sit not quite
alone at the bar, where suits brought by would-be bedmates, paid
and unpaid, sometimes made it difficult to drink in peace.

So Ochin brought back tidbits of gossip: who had been short-
ed by their last employer; who had gotten theirs back, with interest;
who slept together, and who were partnered–entertainment, lightly gotten, and lightly dispensed. These tidbits were shared with
the Commander and Erthax, of course, if they felt to him to have
weight or import, or held in reserve by him to compare with his
plays if they were worthy of extra consideration. Several of his ta-
bleside stories were not only recent but notable–and potentiality
verifiable–those he'd share when he was sure of them.

Pilot Erthax was bolder. He enlisted in contests of small skills:
darts, foot-races, and the like, though he withheld himself from
both drinking games and gambling–which Vepal admitted surprised him. He had been bolder on other stations, before he'd become so challenging to command.

The pilot's information tended to detail mischief and darker deeds: Who had stolen a comrade's favorite blade, and in retribution for what imagined or genuine slight. Who enjoyed the commander's favor; who was on his last probation—and for what cause.
. .

What neither heard was news of the mission, though occasionally one or another would mention that commander this-or-that had gotten his price, and signed in blood, as the inevitable phrasing went, on the Liaden's dotted line.

Vepal's own impression was that there was a certain tension with regard to those signings. The wisdom among the common troops was that, while the promised payments might seem very fine on paper; the recruiting agents were, in large measure, Liaden, and the contract surely so. There would be a clause, a comma, or phrase in that document somewhere, so fretted the common troop, which would, in the end, rob them of their pay.

Occasionally, one would speculate upon the identity of the target, but those idle wonderings were, according to both Ochin and Erthax, and by Vepal's own observation, shut down forcefully with a snarled, "Ain't sapposa talk on that. Commander says, no chatter! Next wise wonderer gets their head bust, 'member it!" from a sergeant or an elder-in-troop—and the conversation would momentarily pause before veering off onto the safer topics of sex—prior or desired—or battles fought long ago.

#

JinJee Sanchez continued to await the arrival of her co-commander, which event she anticipated loudly whenever she and Vepal met, which was surprisingly often.

Commander Sanchez had many associates on station, and she called on them all, frequently attended, at her express invitation, by Vepal.

"Commander Vepal awaits clearance from his commanders at Temp Headquarters," she told those acquaintances. "When he is given leave to sign the NDA, then will we all be kindred in arms. Now is not too soon to learn each other."

To Vepal's surprise, this argument carried force. None of the commanders he met in this way displayed any particular dismay at meeting an Yxtrang commander, though all of those who had signed the NDA, without exception, showed a tight-lipped distress, and a uniform refusal to talk about Perdition Enterprises's plans, even in the most general of terms.

When no one to whom she was personally known was available to receive her, JinJee called upon those she knew by reputation—the details of those reputations being supplied by her colleague, the commander of all secrets. On those days, she and Vepal would meet afterward, to share a beer, and often a meal, while she briefed him on what she had learned.

This shift, she arrived with a grin on her face, fingers up to bespeak two beers even as she slid onto the seat across from him. They were again at *The Headless Yxtrang*, by far their favorite meet-place, though by no means the only one.

"Have you news from your co-commander?" he asked her, that being the most likely public reason for such overt delight.

"No! The bastard sends no word past *urgent business*! I will sell tickets to his public skinning, when he finally sets boots on this station."

The beers arrived. They raised the glasses in one gesture and each took a hearty swallow.

Vepal put his glass down.

"But something has happened to please you," he said.

"Oh, yes; very much, but will it please *you*, is what I ask myself!"

"Does that matter?" he asked, watching her eyes sparkle.

"Improbably, it does, as it involves you most particularly."

"Then you had better tell me," he said. "If my honor is at risk, I must make answer."

"Now, there is where you give me cause for concern!" she said, but laughing as she spoke. She raised her glass and had another swallow.

Vepal, seeing how it was with her, brought two fingers into the air, even as he drained his own glass.

"I will tell you," she said, when the second beers had arrived, and the empties taken away. She put her elbows on the table, and leaned close. He did as well, bending until their heads nearly touched.

"Our frequent meetings have come to the attention of my command, who I doubt you hold in much esteem, given your introduction to many of them."

"The unit is the reflection of the commander," he murmured. "They had forgotten themselves, but recalled quickly enough, when you came among them."

She paused, head tipped, as if struck by this.

"You give me hope, then, that you will find my news as diverting as I do. The more incorrigible of my command have started a pool, Comrade, wagering on the shift and the hour in which we two shall. . .seek out a more private venue, for, let us say, a most intimate meeting."

It took him a moment to understand her, and when he did, he feared that she would feel the heat of the blood rushing into his face.

She shifted, and put her fingers on his wrist–cool fingers against his heated flesh.

"I have offended," she said. "Forgive me, Comrade. Among us it is. . .an indication of acceptance, and in this case, I confess, somewhat of pride, that their commander might conquer an Yxtrang."

He cleared his throat.

"You have not offended," he managed, hearing the growl in his voice, and hoping that she put it down to his obvious embarrassment. "It is done . . .differently among us. Wagers are made on . . .displays of skill and matches of strengths."

A small pause; briefly, she pressed his wrist, then withdrew her fingers.

"Not so much different, then," she said lightly, and leaned back into the seat, reaching for her glass. "If I call for two of today's special, will you share a meal with me?"

He straightened, settling his shoulders against the back of the bench, and met her eyes–raptor bright and fearless. The knot in his stomach loosened.

"I would be proud to share a meal with such a comrade," he said.

#

"Sir."

Erthax rose from the command chair and saluted as Vepal came onto the bridge, itself surprising enough that he checked his progress. ·

"Permission to speak, sir," Erthax said.

Vepal considered saying no, which really was unworthy, before granting permission with the wave of a hand.

"An open message from Recruiter ter'Menth arrived while you were gone, sir, demanding that you attend her at the Core Conference Center at your first free moment. Only give her name at the desk, and she will see you immediately."

The intent of the message was, Vepal strongly suspected, phrased by Erthax in order to give maximum offense. That aside, the message–or one very like it–was not unexpected. One might quibble that a mere recruiter had insufficient rank to order a commander to her, but he was prepared to overlook the slight to what a Liaden would term his *melant'i*, specifically because he wanted no one of Perdition Enterprises to set boots on his decks. A meeting at the conference center therefore suited him well.

"Is there more?" he asked Erthax.

"That is the whole of it," the pilot admitted. "The original is on-screen, if you wish."

"No, I have no need. Archive it. I go."

There was a stir at the hatchway. Vepal turned his head to see Ochin, dressed for duty.

"Escort, sir?"

Clearly Erthax had shared the news of the message with his underling, if only to demonstrate how low the ambassador had fallen to obey an open summons made by a mere flunky, and a Liaden flunky at that.

Vepal might have simply said no, but it was his habit to show the Rifle his reasoning, when possible, so that he might perform his duty the better.

"Not for this. The recruiter is Liaden, and might think that we are escalating a situation which, by the tenor of her message, she already considers difficult."

He saw Ochin consider and reject that reasoning, but the Rifle made no argument. Naturally not. He merely saluted, and stepped to one side, clearing Vepal's path to the hatch.

"Sir."

#

The sound of the hatch closing had not quite faded away when the Rifle looked at the Pilot, and the Pilot glanced briefly down at his board.

"All right," he said, as if the other had said it aloud. "Go watch your Liaden plays. I'll escort-at-a-distance since he always sees you, anyway. Lock down until he's back."

#

As it happened, Vepal had not been required to ask for ter'Menth at the command desk; the recruiter was sitting in one of the chairs in the common room, and rose promptly when he entered.

"Commander, how good of you to come so quickly," she said, teeth showing behind her smile.

"Your message carried some urgency," he answered, smiling in kind. "Naturally, I came as soon as I was aware."

"You honor me," she told him, which he took leave to doubt. "Come, there is an empty room just here . . ."

She bowed him in ahead of her, another small cubicle such as the one where he had first met her. He took the chair nearest the door, as he had on that first occasion, while she passed behind the desk, and arranged herself there.

She did not glance at the screen; perhaps it was blank; perhaps she had no need.

"I regret that I must ask," she said, folding her hands on the desk top before her, "however, those whom I report to are becoming . . .restless."

"I understand," he assured her. "Ask without offense."

She inclined her head.

"We wonder when you might hear from the High Command at Temp Headquarters. Interest in bringing a conquest corps into our expedition remains keen, but there are schedules to maintain, and, as we are both aware, there is only so long that a project of this scope can be kept quiet."

He had, Vepal thought, expected this question. They were after all nearing the end of their week's berthing, and there had been no response—to either of his queries.

"I cannot predict with any accuracy when the commanders may choose to speak," he told her, which was the utter truth. "Understand, not only have Perdition Enterprises asked them to commit on the—your pardon—sketchiest of details, but the request for commitment is, of itself, unique. You will know from dealing with your own command structure that a new situation must be examined from all sides. It might, perhaps, speed their deliberations, if more details were made available to them."

"I understand you, I think," she said, blandly. "Like you, I am constrained by the orders of my superiors. I will therefore take your request to them."

"I'm grateful," he told her.

She moved a hand, perhaps sweeping away his gratitude–or perhaps, he told his rising temper, it meant some other thing altogether, and was nothing near an insult. He did best to let it pass.

"I see you about often with Commander Sanchez of the Paladin mercenary unit. I wonder–forgive me if I am forward–how you come to know her."

Vepal felt the hairs on the back of his neck rise. Had they come now to the real reason for this interview? Still, there was nothing, as far as he could parse the matter–nothing at all wrong with telling the truth.

He therefore did just that: the arrival of the Paladins at the speakeasy on Seebrit Station while Vepal and his small troop were at mess; the threats, the subsequent arrival of Commander Sanchez, and the quick restoration of peace and order.

"We met again, by chance, later that evening, and took the opportunity to talk, as commanders will between themselves. We found ourselves to be in agreement on several topics of importance to us both, and, I believe, we were each dismayed when our separate duties required that we part. I was surprised, but pleased, to find her–a comrade, as it were–here among all of these worthy strangers."

He paused, and gave ter'Menth a nod.

"She has been useful to me. Sanchez knows many commanders, and has introduced me to them. If these soldiers will eventually be fighting shoulder to shoulder with Yxtrang, it is better for all that they learn to know an Yxtrang."

"I see. A most beneficial relationship. And, yet, she confines herself to the commanders of mercenaries, even those previously unknown to her. I wonder that she has not continued her work among our other recruits, who might also benefit from her acquaintance, and yours."

This, thought Vepal, was an odd turn of direction, but candor continued to seem his best course.

"I believe she does not wish to intrude herself, having no acquaintance among those to ease her way as she eases mine."

"Doubtless you are correct," ter'Menth said, and rose, her hands flat on her desk. "Perhaps I shall make it my business to mend that situation for her."

It was said as blandly as any other thing she had said to him, yet Vepal was suddenly certain that the manner of that meeting would be to JinJee's peril.

He trusted that his face did not betray his unease as he rose and bowed slightly from the waist before he left the interview room.

CHAPTER FOUR

Vepal gained the business concourse through the airlock open wide enough to march a parade through and walked in the vague direction of their docking, his pace brisk, but not over-hasty. As he walked, he reviewed the meeting with Recruiter ter'Menth, and failed to find less reason for the concern that still taxed him. There had been nothing overtly *said*–ter'Menth, after all, was Liaden–but the manner of what had *been* said, and what had *not* been said, especially that last, almost absent-sounding comment–

Perhaps I should make it my business to mend that situation for her.

Of course, Recruiter ter'Menth, who was, in his opinion, no mere recruiter, nor had ever intended him to suppose her so–Recruiter ter'Menth most naturally had warriors at her beck. Not merely because there were those who had signed the NDA form, and were therefore subject to the orders of Perdition Enterprises, transmitted through their appointed operatives, but simply because Recruiter ter'Menth was the sort who would be certain to arm herself, as a matter of course.

JinJee Sanchez, now: interminably awaiting her co-commander, making her calls, asking her questions. It might, Vepal thought–it might very well make sense for Recruiter ter'Menth–or, rather say, Perdition Enterprises–to make an example, for the good of discipline. Through her own efforts, JinJee was well-known on station. The Paladins were not the least-counted among those mercenary units on-station; no easy targets, commander or unit.

Vepal entered a lift, and directed it to the food hub. No surprises there, for any who had happened to follow him; the food hub was a favorite destination of his, even when he was not scheduled to meet JinJee.

He stepped off the lift and crossed immediately to the comm-bank, keeping good watch as he called the ship, relaying to Ochin that he was delayed, and would call again when he was on approach to their docking.

That done, he slipped back into the crowd, still keeping a close watch for followers.

He was fortunate in his hour, one of the food hub's busiest. It would not be easy to trail a single man–even a large and distinctive man–through such a crush.

He was also fortunate that the Paladins were housed quite near to the food hub. He might arrive quickly to speak with JinJee regarding the potential threats to the security of herself and her troop.

Of course, there was no need to track him in order to bring mischief down upon the Paladins. ter'Menth knew as well as he where they camped. Vepal's hope lay in the. . .probability that it would take time for any orders ter'Menth issued to be received and acted upon.

He hoped he was wrong, and that his error would become a very good joke between JinJee and himself, down a long future.

In the meantime, he would watch her back, as she watched his.

* * *

Recruiting Agent ter'Menth returned to the common room as a very tall soldier in grays reached the receptionist's desk, and stated in an odd accent, "I want to see Recruiting Agent ter'Menth."

"Do you have an appointment?" the receptionist asked.

"I do not, but the recruiting agent will want to see me, and to hear what I say."

The receptionist was not, of course, a fool, and even if so, his orders contained the fact that ter'Menth was the single contact-point for Yxtrang. Still, there was some value in maintaining the proprieties, especially as this particular Yxtrang was new to the common recruitment area.

"May I tell Recruiting Agent ter'Menth your name and rank?" the receptionist asked calmly.

ter'Menth saw the Yxtrang soldier stiffen; apparently he considered the question impertinent. In the next instant, however, he had gathered himself into hand, and produced a very credible bow.

"I am Erthax Pilot, of Vepal's Small Troop."

Ah, thought ter'Menth, this might in fact be something interesting. She stepped forward, claiming the receptionist's attention with a wave.

"Here is the recruiting agent, now," the receptionist said, obedient to the cue. He stood up and bowed to ter'Menth's honor.

Pilot Erthax hesitated a moment, possibly at a loss for an appropriate form. ter'Menth inclined slightly from the waist, which he took up immediately, reproducing her bow precisely, which a Liaden would see as having declared them equals. Rather than lesson him sternly she took it as a sign that he had not been fully briefed by his commander, so she smiled, showing the teeth a little.

"Pilot Erthax," she said smoothly. "I had not anticipated your arrival. It happens, however, that I am at leisure, and eager to hear what you have to say to me. If you will follow, there is a room just down here where we may be private."

She moved her hand, showing him the direction, and waited until he had stepped around the receptionist's desk, and followed her from the hall.

* * *

At another time the place might have been used for a trade show; what it did now was hold many troops in close quarters. Vepal's ID card as a commander of troops allowed him entry to the area, JinJee being yet true to her open-camp philosophy.

The Paladins had been mustered for inspection, and they made a brave showing, Vepal thought, pausing at the edge of the impromptu parade ground. Leathers and weapons gleamed in the station-light. Shoulders back, faces soldierly, eyes front, the troops stood motionless, scarcely seeming to breathe, as their commander made her leisurely way up and down the lines.

If her troop was brave, JinJee Sanchez was proud; a commander's commander, conducting a meticulous inspection. She paused before one troop, frowning down at his boots. Spoke, too low for Vepal to hear—a private matter, between commander and soldier. The man's fair face colored to a bright red, but he replied with dignity, eyes front. She spoke again, and his *Yes, Commander!* rang over the field, as she moved on to the next, hands behind her back, face grave and thoughtful.

Vepal stood at the sidelines at parade rest, and waited for duty to be done.

* * *

Pilot Erthax sat on the edge of the chair, back straight, both feet on the floor. A pilot on the edge of action, in fact. Agent ter'Menth allowed him to remain so, while she played at tidying things away on the blank screen before her. He was, she thought, rather more patient than she had supposed he would be; though his control over his expression was not nearly so fine as Vepal's. Still, it was to be expected; that command should be the ideal to which all lesser troops must aspire.

"So," she said, without, yet, fully looking at him; "you are come behind your commander's back, to make your own arrangement with Perdition Enterprises?"

There was a moment of charged silence. She heard him take a hard breath.

"You would have me to be without honor," he said, "but you have not yet heard what I have to say."

"Then speak," she said, meeting his eyes squarely. "I will listen until–ah, until I grow bored, does that seem just to you? When I am bored, I will call your commander and desire him to take you into his care."

Interestingly, he laughed, a soft, disdainful sound.

"That is fair, recruiter of soldiers. I will speak quickly, not to risk you growing bored by the sound of my voice."

Another breath, as if to prepare himself for a long speech, which he began, keeping his gaze locked with hers.

"Commander Vepal does not have the ear of the High Command. He is *malkonstituita*–scorned, impotent. A laughing-stock, as I think the phrase may go. If you wish to deal with the High Command, and I think you do, you will need someone whose messages they read; and whose advice they listen to."

"And this would be you?"

He did not move his eyes from hers.

"Yes."

"I seem to recall that Commander Vepal is an ambassador be-tween the Yxtrang and the whole rest of the universe," she said, watching him closely.

He laughed again.

"Oh, he is that! He is a Hero, and a fool, and because he is the first, he cannot be executed for the second. So, he was given a title, and a mission, and sent away; High Command hoping that the universe would kill him, sooner than late. Me, they set to watch him, and to report his actions. If you want to send a message to the High Command, Recruiting Agent, you need me."

It did seem as though the pilot was telling the truth. However.
. .

"I recall that Commander Vepal sent two high security mes-sages from this station, bound for Temp Headquarters."

"He did, yes. They were decoys. I have the texts here."

He reached to the pouch on his belt, and pulled out two thin sheets of hard copy.

"All of his messages are copied to my files," he told her, putting the papers on the desk before her.

She glanced down, but of course could not read them.

"I will need to have these translated, but for the moment, let us suppose that you will tell me what they say."

"Yes."

He tapped the first page.

"This addresses the Finance Officer on the matter of short pay-ments to our expedition." He glanced up at her, and smiled, teeth very apparent.

"You see that he has no standing. The Troop does not cheat the Troop."

"I am informed," she said, truthfully. "And this next one?"

"That is to the Records Officer, inquiring after the current roster of High Commanders."

"So it may be that he strives to do what he was asked," said ter'Menth, "but merely wishes to ensure that he addresses the correct authority."

"Possibly. But he might have also sent a high-security message to the Secretary of Council, who would have distributed it to the High Command."

"I see. So, stipulate that Commander Vepal is stalling, and is not dealing with honor. What do *you* want?"

Another toothy smile.

"I want to help you. I will send your message to the Secretary of Council."

"So kind," she said, blandly. "And in return for this, you will want—what?"

"A command," he said promptly, which did not surprise her, "the ship I pilot–" here he paused, as if coming to agreement with himself. "And Vepal."

Certainly, it was a bargain she could make, with very little chance of damage to herself or the mission. She inclined her head.

"I accept your assistance and your terms," she told him. "Payment upon receipt of a reply from High Command."

"I agree," he said.

"Good. You may use the sealed unit in this facility to send your message. I will give you the text."

His look of extreme satisfaction faded a little.

"Better it is sent from the ship, with the proper equipment."

"No, I insist that you use our equipment. Forgive me, but this ship of yours seems not in the least secure. *My* equipment does not leak."

He thought a moment, then thrust his chin forward.

"Yes," he said. "I am ready now."

"Excellent," she said. "Allow me to call my expert, so that there will be no misunderstanding regarding the message, and then we two will repair to the comm center."

* * *

Inspection ended, and the Paladins were dismissed. JinJee Sanchez strolled over to him. Vepal was aware of many eyes on her–*on them*–and recalled the troop's wager. His ears burned, but he kept his face soldierly, and his demeanor everything that a commander should display before a valued colleague.

"Vepal," she said, reaching his side. "I am happy to see you." She paused, searching his face, and put her hand on his arm.

"What is wrong?"

He glanced around at the multitude of bright, interested eyes, not all of which dropped modestly when his gaze crossed theirs.

"Possibly nothing is wrong," he said, returning his attention to her scarred, strong face. "But I would like to discuss the matter with you. . .in a more private setting."

That may have been misphrased; he heard one of those nearest repeat. . .*a more private setting* and turn sharply to her mate. JinJee heard, surely, the corner of her mouth lifted in a half-smile.

"I will be pleased to be private with you," she said, her voice pitched to be heard by the farthest soldier. Vepal wished he could share her amusement, but the worry that had brought him here was stronger than when he had left Recruiter ter'Menth.

"Come," he said brusquely, and turned back in the direction of the food hub, JinJee at his side. "To our regular table, I think."

She walked beside him, smile deepening at the sound of stealthy footsteps behind them.

"Did you wager as well?" Vepal asked her, with some bitterness.

She shot an amused glanced up into his face.

"I, wager? For shame, Comrade. You know as well as I do that commanders must withhold themselves from such public displays."

She paused briefly, and added, as one being fair.

"Of course, nothing prevents one from wagering with oneself. Does it?"

He was, for a moment, diverted—and a moment was everything that they needed.

There were six of them, in leather, guns belted, blades out.

"Keep 'im occupied; we'll take her," was the growled order, barely heard over the thunder of their boots on decking and a shout that was perhaps meant to freeze him with terror.

Vepal roared, to show them how it was done, and swept out an arm, knocking the nearest of his three against the wall, where he struck with a boom, and slid to the deck, head lolling, knife fallen from lax fingers.

The second made the error of leading with her knife. He broke her wrist, took the blade away, and thrust her, too, against the wall. She struck with a cry, and also slid to the deck, no more than dazed, by Vepal's estimation, but with the fight gone out of her.

The third—but the third was abruptly removed from his consideration by a merc in gleaming leathers, who disarmed the attacker handily, snaked an arm around his neck, and brought him to his knees on the deck.

Vepal spun, but JinJee's attackers were in like case, scattered like so many fallen batons on the deck. Several of the Paladins moved among them, retrieving weapons and applying restraints.

"This one's awake, Commander," said the soldier who had taken Vepal's third. She gave him a conscious look.

"Sorry to spoil your fun, sir."

He considered her, found the humor at the edge of her face, and gave her a nod.

"Not at all," he said courteously. "It would have been rude to keep them all for myself."

The shadow humor blossomed into a grin, and she hauled her prisoner 'round on his knees as Commander Sanchez arrived to look down upon him.

"Orburt Vinkleer," she said.

He grinned, showing a gap between his teeth.

"Hi, JinJee. Lookin' fine."

She did not return the compliment.

"Did you mean to attack myself and Commander Vepal, or are you merely drunk?"

"Orders," he said, his grin widening. "Just followin' orders, zackly like a bought 'n paid for merc."

"Whose orders?"

His grin became a laugh.

"Why would I tell you that?"

"Why wouldn't you? A solid client roster must be to your benefit, as you seek. . .legitimate work."

"Signed the NDA, didn't I?"

"Did you? Will your commander be angry, that you failed in your mission?" She glanced about them, before returning to Orburt Vinkleer.

"At least, I assume that this was not the outcome you envisioned."

"Just showing what happens to them who don't sign on nor get out. Little demonstration for the other hanger-ons."

"Ah, I see." She considered the man, and suddenly snapped out. "What is the target?"

"Like to know, wouldn't cha?"

"In fact, I would; wouldn't you?"

He made as if to shrug, an action his restraints made difficult.

"S'long's they pay me, I don't care who we hit."

"Of course not," JinJee said politely. "Very well, Orburt. My soldiers will escort you to your quarters. Try anything like this again, and you will be returned in a body bag. This may be a game to you, but we are professionals."

She nodded at the soldier holding the prisoner.

"Get them out of here," she said. "No need to be gentle."

"Yes, Commander," said the soldier, and yanked Orburt Vinkleer to his feet.

Others moved, grabbing the downed fighters and throwing them ungently into field carries. Vepal and JinJee watched them out of sight; he very much aware of the four Paladins flanking them, at a respectful distance, and also of the glow along his nerves, the feeling of power rising in his muscles; the first signs of the euphoria. The little skirmish had been enough to waken biology, but not enough to finish it.

He took a breath. He was an Explorer. He was in command of biology.

Teeth set, he bowed his head, and spread his hands.

"My apologies," he said to JinJee; "I came to warn you of this possibility."

She considered him, silent, her expression speculative. It came to him suddenly that the possibility that he had come specifically to guide her into this trap fell well within the bounds of logic. He took a breath, and met her eye.

"I did not," he said, "think that anything would happen so—soon."

"I see," she said then, and gave him a nod.

"I would like to hear what it was you were going to tell me before we were interrupted," she said, then. "I wonder if you will join me in my quarters? On board our ship."

For him, this was a test, Vepal thought. For JinJee, it was an extra measure of security.

He nodded, feeling the telltale shiver in his blood. Taking another breath, he refused the euphoria of battle. He was civilized; he was rational. There was nothing, any longer, for him to fight.

"I'll be pleased to attend you in your quarters, Comrade."

* * *

"The Commander has not returned," Ochin Rifle stated. He did not say the rest of it; could not say the rest of it, as Erthax outranked him. But it was plain for any of the Troop to hear, unvoiced as it was.

Erthax had failed. He had failed his duty to the ship and to the commander.

He, however, Erthax thought, was not a Rifle. He was a pilot; his wits were quick, and his ability to spin a tale far superior to anything that the Rifle might produce. The Rifle was limited to statements of fact, no matter how damning. Erthax was able to be. . .*creative.*

"The Commander has not returned," he agreed. "He saw me, and he was very much displeased. He ordered me back to the ship.

We are to lock down until he arrives, which he will do when, in his sole judgment, it is time to do so."

Ochin frowned.

"You were clumsy," he said—a reinterpretation of what Erthax had told him. Not fact.

"You think the commander is so inept he wouldn't have seen me?" he answered, certain that it would be hours before Ochin could untwist himself from *that*.

"You were clumsy, because you did not convince him to have you, even when you were both already out." Ochin pulled himself up, and looked directly into Erthax's eyes.

"I have followed so myself—twice. Both times, he took me, rather than to have me walk the docks alone."

The implication was plain: A mere Rifle had accomplished this, that a pilot had not.

Erthax held onto his temper, which was already frayed. He needed the Rifle, if not to stand with him, than at least to not stand against him.

"You are correct," he said moderately. "I did not try very hard to keep to him, once he had sent me away. My pride was touched, I think."

Ochin did not say what he thought of pride, if, indeed, a mere Rifle might be equipped to contemplate the concept.

"Now that I am here, shamed or not," Erthax continued; "our part is to follow his orders. We should lock down until he arrives."

"Yes," Ochin said after a moment. "That is all that we can do. Now."

There was a pause before he added.

"You should know that in fact the commander called, *before* you returned. The decks are uncertain. We are to remain locked down until he comes back. He will call again when he is on this level, to give us the order to open."

Erthax took a very careful breath. So close to being discovered, then.

"We will obey," he said.

CHAPTER FIVE

Her quarters. . .surprised.

Vepal had expected a soldier's cell; much like his own, on ship, or perhaps a little larger, like his permanent quarters at Temp Headquarters.

He had not. . .imagined that there would be pale cloth draped 'round walls and ceiling, nor a carpet far richer in pattern and in color than any other he had seen on-station.

Muscles aching, he stood at parade rest, watching her cross the room to a small auto-kitchen, and turn to look at him.

"Will you have something to quench the dust of—we can scarcely call it a battle, I think. Perhaps skirmish?"

"Thank you," he said stiffly. "No."

"I see."

She came back, stopping within what had become a comfortable speaking distance between them.

"I suppose that you will refuse a chair, too, until you tell me. So, then, Comrade—tell me."

He bowed, slight and stiff.

"I returned to my ship this evening and learned that Recruiting Agent ter'Menth had called during my absence, demanding that I come to her at my earliest convenience. I went immediately."

He paused to review a distancing exercise, and continued.

"She asked when I might expect an answer from High Command. I made an excuse, and also a bid for more information, which was turned aside. She then came to what seemed to be her core purpose.

"She said that I was often seen in the company of Commander Sanchez, and wondered how we had come to know each other. I told her the circumstances of our first meeting, and added that you were useful both to me and to Perdition Enterprises. By introducing me to merc command, you were creating an opportunity for we who will hopefully soon be united in a glorious mission to gain the measure of our comrades."

He could feel himself shivering with need. If he didn't engage in physical exercise soon, he would collapse in an ignominious heap of cramped muscles. JinJee might then amuse herself by having him delivered to her command's common area, where he might be mocked by all.

"Recruiter ter'Menth made note that you called only on mercs, and not on those who were . . .other. I suggested perhaps that you did not wish to intrude upon them, having no acquaintance among them to ease your way, as you eased mine. It seemed apt enough when I said it, but it appeared to me that it gave her thoughts an odd trajectory. She said, '*Perhaps I shall make it my business to mend that situation for her.*' It made me. . .uneasy, and I came to lay the matter before you, even though I half-believed I was being foolish."

"And now we have learned that you were not foolish at all, and that Recruiting Agent ter'Menth likes to make mischief when she grows bored. Unfortunately, if her goal was to widen my acquaintance, she chose badly–I am *well* acquainted with Commodore Vinkleer. Now."

She crossed her arms over her chest, and sent him a stern look, such as a commander might bend upon a trainee who had failed to enumerate *all* of his weapons.

"I will leave you now," Vepal stated.

"No," she said. "*Now*, you will tell me what ails you, Comrade. Were you struck? If so, you must come with me to our medic. Vinkleer's rabble have been known to doctor their blades, and those who don't never clean them. The chance of infection is not trivial."

"No, I–I must go," he said. He was shivering in earnest now. How he was to achieve his ship in this state, he hardly knew. Yet, to betray himself before JinJee. . .

"No, you must not," she said, command voice snapping hard enough to allow him to gain some control. "You are plainly ill. You will sit down. I will call the medic to–"

"No!"

It was a roar. JinJee raised an eyebrow.

"I–no medic," he managed. "Please. It is–only biology."

A second eyebrow rose.

"How so?"

"The skirmish, as you so aptly put it," he said. "It was long enough to trigger a–a release of. . .specialized hormones. However, it was neither long enough nor violent enough to burn them. If I do not act–soon–my muscles will cramp and I will be unable. . ."

"What is the antidote?" she snapped.

"Physical release. Perhaps I might spar with one of the troop. Or–"

"The punching bag," she said, in a tone of enlightenment. "I understand."

She smiled then, and stepped closer to him.

"I offer, Comrade, physical release. Will you accept?"

He had no choice; he would never make it across the docks. JinJee was able, as he had just seen demonstrated, and he was not out of control; he had never been one for the full battle frenzy.

"Yes," he told JinJee Sanchez; "I accept."

#

He woke all at once, which was his habit, and took stock, eyes closed, which was also his habit.

A tantalizingly familiar scent enveloped him; the scent of Jin-Jee Sanchez, that was, entwined with others, less familiar. The surface he lay on was firm, but not so firm as his pallet on-ship. Against his left side was pressed a long warmth, which shifted even as he noted its presence.

He recalled—last night's attack, the unfortunate triggering of the battle frenzy; JinJee's offer of physical release.

. . .a release which had not at all been what he had expected, though. . .effective, nevertheless.

Very effective.

"You are awake, Comrade?" her voice was much as always, and he smiled, at other memories.

"I am awake, Comrade," he replied. He hesitated, and added, "Thank you."

"I do not believe," said JinJee Sanchez, shifting so forcefully that he opened his eyes, and looked up into her face, as she leaned over him, the lean muscles of her torso on full display, "that I wish to enter into a protracted conversation of who is more grateful to whom. We both benefited, and I am neither thankful nor sorry."

Black raptor's eyes; the mark of the war blade's kiss a potent reminder of her strength. He felt the stirrings of last night's passions, in which the action they had engaged upon had seemed something more than the mere comfortable coupling of comrades.

"What are you then?" he asked her, even as he wondered after his own emotions.

"I am *pleased*," JinJee said, with a long smile. She threw back the blanket which had covered them both, exposing him in full display.

"Also," she said, gripping him in one strong hand while she met his eyes boldly; "I am eager, as I see that you are. Shall we, again?"

He lifted one hand to her scar; the other to her breast, and smiled into her bold, warrior's eyes.

"Yes," he said. "Let us, again."

#

They came arm and arm into the Paladin's mess, amid shouting and applause. Attuned to her movements, Vepal paused with her, looking over the pandemonium until it had quieted. Only then did they continue to the commander's table, where a second chair had been hastily placed, and a second place laid.

They being among her command, Vepal waited to take the second chair until she was seated.

A soldier guided a serving tray to their table. A steaming cup of brown liquid was set before JinJee before the server looked to him, his hand fluttering between pots and carafes.

"Your pleasure, sir? We have coffeetoot, Terran tea, citrus juice, berry juice, water."

"Coffeetoot," Vepal told him, and while it was being poured, JinJee asked.

"Who won?"

"McGyver and Hayashi split, ma'am."

JinJee put her cup on the table.

"Take them each my compliments," she said, "and collect the five percent for the medical fund."

"Hayashi put in already, ma'am. Sergeant Pillay's gone to collect from Mac."

"All in hand, then," JinJee said. "We'll serve ourselves, Thaydo, thank you."

"Yes, ma'am. Sir."

The soldier saluted and left them.

"There is," JinJee said, continuing the discussion they had begun in her quarters, "safety in numbers. While none of us are safe from ambush, you and your small troop, my friend, are considerably more at risk than I, or any of mine. We can double up, offer you guard– "

"We hardly present a menace, all three walking the deck together," he finished for her, and added, privately: Even supposing that Erthax would not wait that one telling heartbeat before leaping to his commander's defense.

Which surely no one but a fool would suppose. Still–

"We have already purchased Recruiter ter'Menth's interest," he pointed out.

"You make my point for me," she answered, and looked up from her meal.

"Understand, I do not wish to absorb you. Your command will remain your command. My command will remain mine. We will be allies, which we have already shown ourselves to be, merely cementing our position."

"I will think on it," he said. "There is a thing that Liadens say, about putting all the wine in one cellar. . ."

She laughed, and shook her head.

"Indeed, indeed. However, if we are basing decisions upon Liaden proverbs, it is also said that an ally is better than a cantra-piece."

Vepal laid his fork down, and met her eyes.

"These Liadens are very talkative."

Another laugh, this one softer.

"That does seem to be so. Well! You will think, and I will await the outcome of your thought. In the meantime, the Paladins will double-up in the common areas. We will no longer put our trust in the station's perimeter alarms."

"You don't ask my permission for these things," he said, "or my agreement."

"No," she agreed, calmly, "I don't."

He drank off the last of his coffeetoot, and pushed back from the table.

"I to my ship, for now," he said, standing.

JinJee also stood, and extended her hand. He took it, and they exchanged a brief pressure. The room had grown very quiet.

"Until again," JinJee said loud enough to reach every ear.

"Until again," he responded, and bowed slightly over their joined hands before slipping free and leaving her, amidst silence.

The moment he cleared the mess hall door, cheering broke out, and a chant which seemed to be only her name: "JinJEE JinJEE JINJEE!" Followed by a roar.

Vepal smiled.

After all, what more was there to add?

#

He was not so fortunate in his hour this shift; the food hub was all but deserted, and he was perfectly visible to the small figure who moved casually, or so it seemed, to intersect his course.

He could perhaps have lost her; his stride was twice as long as hers. But that would have been pointless, besides showing an unwillingness to be forthcoming and cooperative.

Vepal slowed his pace.

"Good-day to you, Recruiting Agent ter'Menth."

"And to you, Commander Vepal. I am pleased to see that you suffered no ill-effects."

He looked down at her, but her face was averted.

"Ill-effects," he repeated. "From what should I have suffered ill-effects?"

Recruiter ter'Menth was not put off her stride in the least. The look she cast up into his face might be said to express amusement.

"Doubtless the affair was so trivial it escaped your notice," she said. "I speak of the report of an altercation between certain operatives of the Vinkleer Cooperative and yourself and Commander Sanchez."

"Oh," Vepal said, still slightly puzzled; "that."

"Indeed. *That*. An unfortunate event, to be sure. However, I was pleased to note that all sides worked together to reach a mutually satisfactory solution. One only hopes that Commander Sanchez's co-commander arrives soon, so that we may welcome her and her company entirely into our ranks."

"I believe she anticipates his arrival daily."

"Yes, so I have heard. Repeatedly. Well! It was, as I said, good to meet you, Commander, and to see you in such robust good health. I will leave you here, and bid you good-day."

"Good-day," Vepal said, and paused for a moment to watch the Liaden depart, and the manner of it. She walked light; she walked alert; and for all her lack of size she walked as if she owned the Inago Station and every life on it.

Which was, Vepal thought, resuming his own stride, a rather disquieting thought, at the least.

CHAPTER SIX

Vepal woke, and lay, eyes closed, and body relaxed, questing after that which had wakened him.

Even as he did so, it came again; a small exhalation, as of air being released, or throttled.

Air. Being throttled.

It had come, he thought. Erthax had received his order to end the mission. It was ironic, perhaps, that it came now.

He took a deep breath, filling his lungs; recalling the breather he had placed in his command locker, years ago, upon taking his first measure of Erthax.

He rolled off his cot, dropped silently to the floor, extended a long arm, placed his fingertips against the lock. . .and a moment later the breather was around his neck, ready for use.

The hiss of whistling air came again, which was unnecessary. The air could have been evacuated from this compartment, very quickly, if not noiselessly, via the control panel in the main hall. There was no need to come to his very quarters, to release the air manually. Erthax certainly knew that. But Erthax didn't want him to die quickly, Vepal thought. Oh, no; Erthax wanted him to know what was happening. Erthax wanted to toy with him, as if he were *kojagun*–prey–rather than a true soldier of the Troop.

Oh, foolish.

Vepal rose to his feet, his blood warming agreeably.

One short stride brought him to the door. He pressed against the wall, making himself as small a target as possible, and triggered the release.

The door opened, which surprised him. Even a man drunk on revenge might think to destabilize the relative pressures sufficiently to seal the door.

He trust his foot in the track so that the door would not close, swung out–

"I yield!" Ochin Rifle whispered, urgently. "Commander. . ."

Vepal blinked, grabbed the Rifle by the collar and hauled him inside, releasing the door as he did so.

"Explain yourself!" he snapped.

Ochin saluted, standing at attention.

"Sir. Pilot Erthax received a communication, sir. From High Command. Security wrap, and the Secretary's seal. I saw it, and I saw that he did not call you. Sir. Therefore, I stepped aside, where I could watch the Pilot, though I could not read the screens. He read the message, then rose and went to quarters. Sir. I thought–you should know."

Vepal considered him. The Rifle was a truthful man–how could he be otherwise? Though this tale did much, he realized, to call his simplicity into question. Whether it was a fabrication or the truth; the Rifle's actions had been extraordinary.

And if the whole tale had been given him by Erthax to tell out again to Vepal? But what would be the purpose of that?

"At ease," he told Ochin.

He went to his private console, and opened the message queue. The last message there was from station, reminding them that they would be required to depart, or move their docking inside of the next twenty-six Standard Hours, or face fines.

"This message," he said over his shoulder to Ochin; "when did it arrive?"

"Thirty-three minutes ago, Sir."

So. He had known of Erthax's private account, but he had considered it best to pretend ignorance. And, if indeed this were merely an acknowledgment of a previously filed report–but no. Council high security wrap, and sealed with the Secretary's codes. This had been no mere ack. This was worth accessing, though Erthax would know that his line was no longer secure, nor his operations secret.

On that thought, he brought up the ship plan, finding himself and Ochin in his quarters, and Erthax–

But there was no third heat signature, in Erthax's quarters, nor anywhere else in the ship. Vepal took a deep breath.

The time for subtlety and subterfuge was over.

He was inside of the Pilot's private queue in a matter of moments. High Command's query was brief: An extraordinary message had been received under Erthax's codes, but sent from an unauthorized source. Had Erthax been compromised? Was this message from him? An explanation by return secure pinbeam was.
. .demanded. If, in fact, the message was from Erthax, more details were solicited.

There was no ack in the sent queue. And Erthax was not on the ship.

The matter, Vepal thought, was plain. Erthax had made his bargain with Perdition Enterprises. He had gone to meet his contact, to wrest more detail from them–no, he corrected himself, from *her*. Recruiting Agent ter'Menth, of course, who liked to make mischief when she was bored. He wondered what she had agreed to give Erthax for sending this message–and abruptly straightened, for the answer was obvious, and he must act quickly, on behalf of his own command.

Vepal spun toward the Rifle, standing yet patiently at attention. Ochin Rifle, loyal to his commander—to *his* commander, Vepal saw now; not merely to command.

"You will carry a message to Commander JinJee Sanchez of the Paladin Mercenary Unit," he said sharply. "You will take your kit, and field pack. After delivering the message, you will place yourself under Commander Sanchez's orders. Go, now, and make ready."

"Commander—" Ochin said, astonishing yet again.

Vepal stood forward, and put his hand on the Rifle's shoulder.

"It was well-done, that small hiss of air to wake me. I am pleased with your ingenuity and forethought. A message not to be discovered in the files! You will obey your orders, and you will serve Commander Sanchez as if she were myself. You will at all times protect her as if you are protecting myself and our mission. You are on detached duty; Erthax is no longer in your chain of command, you will not engage with him if you see him. I will recall you when conditions allow."

He removed his hand.

"Go now, and make ready."

Ochin did not like his orders. Very nearly, Ochin protested, a second time, but in the end, he was a Rifle, and Vepal his commander. He saluted, and left, to make ready.

Vepal penned a brief message for JinJee: Here was Ochin Rifle to receive the training Vepal had discussed with her. He trusted she would find him an apt student.

That done, he dressed and armed himself, and went to meet Ochin at the lock.

* * *

Vepal opened one eye and considered the main board, with its one bright yellow tell-tale.

Someone had opened the outer lock.

He opened the other eye and lazily spun the pilot's chair until it faced the open hatchway, and the main hall beyond. His hands were laced over his belt, elbows resting carelessly on the arm controls, and his legs were thrust out before him, crossed at the ankles. The very picture of indolence, with nothing soldierly about him.

A shadow moved at the end of the hall, and here at last came his tardy pilot, walking very lightly–and freezing in surprise to see the hatch unsealed, and Vepal beyond it.

"Well met, Pilot!" Vepal said, showing his teeth in a wide grin. "Come in! I've been waiting to talk with you."

Erthax visibly shook himself and came forward, his tread wary now, and his eyes glinting.

"Commander," he said, sharp enough to fall outside of the line of insolence, and produced a perfunctory salute.

"Pilot." Vepal didn't bother to return the salute. "Was Recruiting Agent ter'Menth forthcoming?"

Erthax did not bother to pretend.

"I have enough for Command," he said, with a sort of sneering certainty.

"Rich pillage?" asked Vepal.

"Yes; and more. A world vulnerable to attack, though occupied by mercenary forces. The Troop stands to gain weapons and materiel, and to rid itself of a considerable number of trained opponents, in one hammer-strike."

Vepal frowned. Such a target *would* appeal to Command. And a mixed invasion force meant that the cost of acquiring these benefits might be attractively low. Command would understand those things very well. As for the contract, Vepal thought—what was a contract to the Troop, to bind them when it was time to strike?

"Coordinates?" he suggested.

"Not yet," Erthax said. "This will be enough."

He grinned again, teeth flashing.

"She gave you to me."

Vepal moved a lazy hand.

"Your price. Naturally. My life, and the Rifle's, and a ship to command. She *did* give you a command?"

"I will have it as soon as the High Commanders send their agreement, and I sign the contract for them." He paused. "I need the Rifle, of course. But you, Commander—you, I do *not* need."

"Recruiting Agent ter'Menth may still have questions for me," Vepal pointed out, watching Erthax's hands.

"Then, she will need to ask them of me," the Pilot said, and there was the gun, in the left hand, arm swinging up—

Vepal punched the control under his elbow; the chair spun hard to the left, as he threw himself to the right.

* * *

Commander Sanchez considered the note, and again considered the soldier who had delivered it. Ochin Rifle, as he named himself. He held himself well, though there was an edge. His orders, so he had told her, received from the commander himself, had been to deliver the note, and to place himself at her word.

He had obeyed his orders, had Ochin Rifle. Plainly, JinJee thought, looking into his eyes, he did not *like* his orders, but he wasn't, after all, required to like his orders, no more than any other soldier.

"In your opinion," she said now; "is Commander Vepal in danger of his life?"

There was a slight hesitancy, before a fist rose to strike the opposite shoulder.

"Commander. Yes, Commander. In my opinion."

"Thank you. Keep with me, Rifle. Abercrombie, Singh, Henshaw, Pike, Latvala–to me, please. We're going for a walk. Sergeant Pillay!"

"Ma'am!"

"Seal up, Sergeant. Disable non-certified personnel seeking to enter our area. Commander Vepal is certified. If he arrives, hold him lightly, and with all respect for his rank–but hold him."

"Yes, ma'am," Pillay said with enthusiasm. He snapped off a very pretty salute, possibly to soothe Ochin Rifle's feelings, and turned, already shouting out the squad list, and protocols.

JinJee shook her head. They'd been at dock too long. They'd all been at dock too long; and it was a major miracle that none of the assembled mercs and pirates hadn't started a war yet, out of simple boredom.

"All right," she said to her squad. "We're going to recover Commander Vepal and give him safe escort to Paladin space. Eyes sharp. With good luck we'll intercept him on his way to us. With bad luck, we'll need to extract him from a Situation, in which case, he could be wounded, even badly wounded. Medic Latvala, stay sharp."

"Yes, ma'am," Latvala answered, sounding positively eager.

JinJee shook her head.

"Let's go."

* * *

Erthax had known nothing beyond what he had initially reported; Vepal had made certain of that. Grisly work, not proper soldiering, but necessary. Once he was sure that there was nothing else, he had used Erthax's own grace blade to end the business, and disposed of the remains before he composed the message to High Command, wrapped in Erthax's codes, and sent from his console.

"Treachery," read the message. "Account terminated. Vepal."

These duties complete, he picked up his field kit and exited the ship, making for the food hub, and beyond.

Of course, he could not remain with the Paladins; he must seem to those who watched him to be going about his usual affairs. Tomorrow, for instance, he would need to find a more appropriate docking for the ship. This off-shift, however. . .

This shift, he wanted, very much, to talk to a comrade, to someone who understood command and the duties of command. He wanted to be in a proper camp, surrounded by proper soldiers, who knew about duty and loyalty, and the price of betrayal.

Also, Erthax's information. JinJee would need it, for herself, and to send on to her colleague, the master of all secrets.

He took the lift to the food hub, which would be very nearly deserted at this station-hour.

But, it was not deserted. He was confronted by a crowd as he exited the lift—and felt a spike of sheer joy at the prospect of a clean fight.

Then he recognized the tallest in the crowd, even as Ochin Rifle called out.

"Commander Vepal, sir!"

"At ease, Rifle," he said, as a less-tall figure separated from the group, and JinJee Sanchez put her hand on his arm.

"All is well, Comrade?" she murmured, for his ears alone.

"Maybe not so well," he answered, just as softly. "We need to talk. I place myself under your protection for this shift and perhaps the next. If you will allow, Commander."

Her fingers tightened on his arm, and she turned, bringing him with her.

"Not only do I allow, I insist," she replied, and raised her voice to address her soldiers.

"We have achieved our goal; and now we return to camp. Singh and Henshaw, take the rear; Abercrombie and Pike on point. Latvala and Rifle, flank us."

She released his arm and brought her weapon out, and Vepal did the same.

"Yes," she said, and gave him a feral grin. "We go."

CHAPTER SEVEN

Two days later, an unassuming lieutenant, or so it would seem, walked into camp during evening mess, presenting credentials which caused her to be conducted without delay to the table where Commanders Sanchez and Vepal were dining together, as had become their wont, and, at JinJee's lightly raised hand, was forthwith given a third chair, a plate, and, at the lieutenant's rather breathless request, a pot of coffeetoot.

"Vepal," JinJee said as the junior officer poured and drank a cup of 'toot straight down. "This is Lieutenant Cheladin. She's attached this mission with the Lyr Cats. She has no manners, as you can see, but she is often entertaining. Chelly. . ."

The lieutenant glanced up, and put her cup gently on the table.

"I apologize for my lack of couth," she said, her voice soft and drawling. "I really did need that, JinJee. Thank you for your forbearance."

"Not at all; I am used to you." JinJee glanced to Vepal. "We took training together," she explained, and looked back to the lieutenant.

"I only worry about the impression you make upon my comrade; he is accustomed to a more rigorous style." She extended a hand and touched Vepal's sleeve.

"Here is Commander Vepal, Chelly. He and his aide Ochin form an auxiliary with us. Nolan is his sergeant, should you have need."

"You don't say! I'd thought Ezra had retired years ago!"

She turned to Vepal.

"Nolan was born a sergeant, sir; you'll get nothing but the best from him. Not that you need me to tell you that."

67

Vepal inclined his head.

"I have already been much comforted by the sergeant's care," he said blandly, and Lieutenant Cheladin grinned.

"Of course you have," she said.

The serving tray arrived at that juncture, and the lieutenant busied herself with choosing foodstuffs.

Vepal, under the guise of giving attention to his own meal, considered the side of JinJee's face.

He had come to know her well; easily well enough to see the worry through the mask of amused tolerance she bent upon her creche-mate as she filled her plate and addressed it with gusto.

"I am of two minds," JinJee said, after the lieutenant had paused long enough to pour and drain another cup of 'toot. "*Do* I want to know why you are here, Chelly?"

The lieutenant sighed, her shoulders softening, and neatly crossed her knife and fork over the negligible remains of her meal.

"No," she said, meeting JinJee's eyes.

"Splendid," JinJee responded. "Then do not tell me."

She raised her hand, and here came the aide to gather up all their plates and offer desert, which, surprisingly, Lieutenant Cheladin declined.

"Let us go for a turn about the camp," JinJee said, pushing back from the table and rising. "I don't think you've seen the new configuration."

"Is this *another* new configuration?" asked her comrade. "By which I mean, the fourth?"

"Such a retentive memory—the fourth, yes. We must keep sharp, you know."

"Then, I'm agog to see the new configuration. I was amazed you managed to get three varies out of this space. Four leaves me speechless."

"As if such a thing were possible," JinJee said amiably. They had reached the door of the mess, which was opened for them by an attentive soldier.

JinJee exited first, followed by Vepal, then the lieutenant, in strict order of rank. Once outside, JinJee turned to the left, and Vepal to the right, where his small command made camp, and where Ochin Rifle stood expectantly at guard by the flagged perimeter.

"No," JinJee said softly. "Vepal, please accompany us."

So, this *was* something more than an old friend at liberty.

Vepal hesitated, glanced at his loyal troop, felt his companions take in his glance.

"I'm seen as remiss if I have no guard," Vepal said with a sigh, "Clearly, two mercenary officers are insufficient honor to my rank."

"I see," JinJee said, "he has been much alone of late, hasn't he? Let him be our honor guard, then."

The ambassador summoned his man.

"Five paces behind, Ochin Rifle. Guard us carefully, as befits a combined command."

Ochin saluted very smartly. "Yes, Commander Ambassador. A combined command."

Vepal fell in at JinJee's right hand; the suddenly sober Cheladin on her left, and they moved out.

"Advance troops were being selected last night," she said, softly, but not making any effort to obscure her words. "They've got to prep their equipment and command structure. They haven't boarded yet. We've got a tracer on them."

"We'd heard Liad was the target; Clan Korval the sponsor," Jin-Jee said.

"I'd heard that one," Chelly said.

"Vepal disagrees with that target, by the way."

"And so?"

Vepal sighed, shook his head vaguely. "These are not warlike people, this Korval, except when pushed. They do not seek trouble. Clan Korval is not on the attack against Liad."

Chelly nodded. "I'll put my coin with the commander's—so then, not Liad."

"Have you anything more likely?"

"I did have a thought. Surebleak might not yet be secure."

There was a small pause, before JinJee murmured.

"In fact, that is Clan Korval's new home world?"

"That's right," Cheladin said.

JinJee waved a hand, taking in, so Vepal surmised, the entire space station, and all the soldiers on it.

"All of this, to dispose of a single Liaden clan?" she said. "They must be formidable."

"They are," said Cheladin. "But they're not necessarily the target. Or maybe only peripherally the target."

"What else, then?" asked JinJee.

"Mercs," said Cheladin succinctly.

"Clan Korval has hired forces? Perdition Enterprises, or whoever is behind it, sees this as a threat to their own agenda?"

"Clan Korval's situation," said the lieutenant, "is unique. I will send files—nothing that Research Officer Aritz couldn't locate in six minutes, and compile in an hour, but I happen to have it all to hand.

"The short form: Korval is exiled from Liad for crimes against the planet. They relocated to Surebleak with, I gather, a strictly limited show of remorse, and a ready plan. Recall, too, that it was Korval that took command of the forces on Lytaxin when the mercs there were blind-sided, and they handed the Fourteenth a thundering loss. There's a fondness for Clan Korval among certain of our brethren, some of whom subsequently assisted in the so-called crime against Liad–under proper contracts, the terms of which were scrupulously kept.

"Also, Clan Korval has chosen for its new base a planet rife with opportunity, in a sector previously thought closed. I've heard that there's a new Merc Intake Center with Recruit Depot planned; they have a sufficiency of uninhabited land in interesting sizes and shapes, as well as a challenging climate."

Vepal bowed slightly in agreement, "This matches my information."

"Rich plunder," said JinJee quietly. "Either the mercs or Clan Korval would not be quite tempting enough. Two such targets in one location, however. . ."

"Becomes irresistible, to a certain type of client."

"Speaking only for myself," JinJee said, "I would give a very great deal to know who is the client."

"Working on it," Cheladin said.

"Warnings have been sent," JinJee said. "Of course."

"Well," Cheladin said, and failed to admit to that case.

JinJee paused, and turned to face her creche-mate.

"Warnings have *not* been sent?"

"We're trying to get the word out, as a hint," Cheladin said, sounding suddenly weary. "I lost a courier–whoever Perdition Enterprises is has the station under tight patrol. I'm afraid we lack our

own pinbeams at the moment due to our civilian docking arrange-
ments, and we dare not assume station pinbeams are secure.."

JinJee took a quiet breath; and another.

"Which," Cheladin said quickly, "is why I'm here. Actually."

"Go on," JinJee said.

"You'll recall that my team, laggards and thrill-seekers as they
are, and thinking themselves above their brethren in arms, on arrival sought for themselves quarters on the civil and residential side
of the station."

"I recall this, of course," JinJee murmured.

"Yes. And you will also recall that I, as officer in charge, made
it my business to seek out station society, particularly the stationmaster and the board of governors. Inago being situated as it is, and
reasonably busy even when not hosting a hiring fair of epic propor-
tion, begin to find, let us say, the peculiar strains placed upon the
station by the presence of the fair to be stretching their expertise.

"Happily, I was in a position to offer the station the use of my
laggard team, most of whom, as you know, are quite knowledge-
able, once they allow themselves to be roused to work."

"Has there been an increase of. . .system stresses, on the civilian
side?" JinJee asked politely.

"Sadly, there have, and though my team has become interested
in the emerging problems, it was suggested that they might need
reinforcements. I thought of you."

"I think," JinJee said quietly, "that it is time for my co-commander to have found us an easy security job on Panore, or perhaps one
of the sea-side worlds at Canova. We'll be striking camp and mov-
ing out tomorrow. I will, myself, call at the recruiting office and for-
mally remove the Paladins from the list. Vepal—how would you?"

Before he could answer, Cheladin spoke again.

"That. . .may not be possible any more, JinJee."

"When I have heard complaint from Recruiting Agent ter'Menth herself that she grows bored with my malingering? I think she would be very glad to see our backs."

A chime sounded, very softly. The lieutenant reached to her belt; raised a communicator to her ear.

"Cheladin," she said quietly, and, on a different note– "Got it. Take precautions."

She clipped the comm back onto her belt, and–said nothing, her gaze seemingly on something beyond the station's horizon, or years in the past.

JinJee placed a careful hand on her friend's arm.

"What happened?"

"An altercation, between forces known and unknown. Two of the Lyr Cats were attacked and injured pretty badly. Preliminary report is they were cornered near the airlock to the civil side, and made it through to aid on that side–but now the airlock's been taken hostage and held, by someone. No firefight, but edged weapons and deadly intent."

JinJee raised an eyebrow.

"We're not visible yet; have to wait for portmaster's response."

JinJee nodded at that, her reply unheard as station hazard klaxons sounded urgently, the red and blue flashes of the warning lights signifying a pressurization problem. Behind them, to their right, curtains of metal slid with a rumble from side walls, and dropped from ceilings with tremendous force, leaving behind them pressure changes and echoes. Rather than an open concourse they stood now in a long hall with small access doors topped by more blinking lights.

The vocal warning in Trade followed quickly: "Airlock issue Deck Seven. Follow standard protocols, Lock Three on emergency seal. Avoid this area. All region airlocks on emergency full seal now. Section airlocks by authorized poll cards only. Refrain from crossing air boundaries until further notice."

There was cussing in several languages as the group heard the news.

"We're on the wrong side of these doors to get back to our command, aren't we?" JinJee asked as everyone checked their weapons. Behind them, Ochin turned in a crouch, on guard, gun in hand, as more distant rumbles and clanks shook the floor, and the station locked down hard.

Chelly unclipped her handheld, pulling up a map.

"There may be a way to get through!"

CHAPTER EIGHT

The large access doors to cross boundary openings were sealed and locked but the doors to the manual stairways were not: Cheladin confirmed that the one across the corridor from the one Ochin experimentally opened was also accesible.

"We can go up or down," she muttered, "but not through!"

Cheladin's fingers ran over the face of the device as she tried another idea, cussed, worked on.

"The stairway lights, Ambassador, are on the battery. Subsystems may not be as well guarded."

"Thank you, Rifle, I hadn't considered that ..."

"Do you think all the units are cut off? Or is this a Perdition operation at work?" JinJee glanced back and forth between the doors held open by Ochin and the lieutenant.

Cheladin pulled another comm from a pocket, punched that into operation–

"Cheladin," she said, "Update. We're on the wrong side, um, here, can you give me directions to anything open?"–and read off the corridor and level markers above the door she leaned against.

"You, too? Check with anyone who'll talk to you, we're going to have to be patient or hike..."

The lieutenant's face showed her worry–

"Stationmaster is going full storm on this, looks like."

Vepal nodded agreement to JinJee, asking both, "Priority? My ship is far enough out on the docking rim to send a pinbeam if you have the coords and trust me to have them. If we need to storm a barricade we may lack the weapons and staffing."

"Wait–I'm getting possible routes–one's up the stairs your man has open," she showed him the screen. " There are routes in red, those are closed. There are routes with blue stars–those are pollways. There's one that's gray–status not known–that's up three decks and should lead to both merc and business sections."

Agreement was instant, with Ochin perforce taking the lead, jumping three stairs at a time with remarkable ease and quiet, gun tucked away on favor of agility. The officers followed, Cheladin mounting the stairs with comm in one hand and gun in the other, the officers using hand grips to speed their way. The stairs were part of an air transport system, grids and grills open.

The sound above of a door slamming, and busy feet; Ochin froze, glancing down to Vepal for guidance.

JinJee signaled pause, and Vepal did too. Ochin took the time to pull a knife from his leg pocket.

No more sound came to them. Had someone been testing a door to see that it would open, or going through one?

Cheladin stretched, hands touching here and there about her person before pulling a tiny item from her belt, considering, and putting it back...

"Gods of guns, who'd think we'd be having this much trouble because of a Liaden no one knows? No record of her in any merc contract histories, none of her organization. It's be one thing if it *was* Korval invading Liad–might be some sense there. But what's to trust this crew, or their contracts? And Korval's no pushover. Korval's not a pushover even for *his* people," she said, nodding toward Vepal. "Did your High Command go for an alliance?"

Ochin laughed from his spot higher on the stairway, startling the officers.

JinJee raised her eyebrows and looked toward Vepal, who spread his hands wide, palm-up, shrugging Terran fashion.

"Please, Rifle," she said, "your thoughts, if the Ambassador permits."

"Indeed," said Vepal, "we are intrigued."

"I think," said Ochin, tucking his laugh away and showing a serious face indeed, "that such a strategic mistake is not likely from the High Command. The lieutenant mentions the defeat of the 14th by Tree-and-Dragon.

"After they routed an enemy on Liad, using their own battleships, Scout ships, and local forces led by Korval's own leaders. Surely they are not without strength, and resource, this Korval."

Ochin paused, head cocked as if listening, then went on...

"This does seem a potential reason for Liaden revenge against Korval."

He paused, gained surety.

"I think, too, that the High Command must know, if even *I* do, that the Clutch are allies of Korval. Did you not know that Korval's very headquarters building from Liad was delivered, in one piece, building and infamous tree, by a Clutch vessel cut from an asteroid?"

He paused, listened to silence yet again, went on.

"The Clutch have weapons no one can stand against. Troop lore tells us of ships of monstrous size appearing at will inside defense rings and absorbing the energy of the strongest beams, and of an invasion where songs sung by five Clutch soldiers brought down walls and destroyed weapons held by Troops. It is said that if a Clutch begins to sing it is safest to throw your weapon far away before it blows up in your hands. "

Ochin turned, looked meaningfully at Vepal.

"The Troop knows, mouth to mouth across the years, that Temp Headquarters itself, within a ring of five defensive moons, could not prevent the landing of a dozen Clutch vessels at Prime Base itself."

Vepal blanched. So much for security and the secrets of command!

Ochin plowed ahead.

"Will the High Command forget this?" He looked them straightly in the eyes then, a man secure in this thoughts.

"For that matter, there are mercenaries here, who fought ... for Korval. A man I spoke to, a Life Sergeant of the Lyr Cats, talked of being on the world called Surebleak when the Tree came down out of space in a rock bigger than Surebleak's biggest city, to be installed at the top of a hill defending the city. So, Command probably knows."

Ochin laughed gently.

"It would be madness to take on this fight, unless it was all for one last shout of honor. We cannot be that desperate, the Troop. Our High Command should not listen to such an offer, for sake of history. Nor should any. I have read many of the *melant'i* plays and seen cites of the history behind them. Attack a world where Korval *is* the line of command and is backed by mercs in place and has these Clutch as allies? Only if the plan is to sing Honor's Song while being destroyed. That I believe, but this is not my decision."

Then a sigh and he continued more quietly.

"In the plays, there is this: what some might call revenge the Liadens call Balance, and this sounds to me like an attempt at that—why not make the mercenaries who fought for Korval fight against them? Why *not* have the Scouts who fought for Korval destroyed fighting mercenaries. Why *not* weaken all of them, this

Surebleak, this Korval ... so that those sitting on Liad can laugh and sweep up what is left without damage to themselves?

"In the most important Liaden plays–friends would fight friends and allies fight allies, all to illustrate proper behavior. And here? If the High Command could be drawn in and the Clutch destroy Temp Headquarters, Liad would be victorious and without enemies."

He was quiet then, Ochin, fully delivered of his thoughts.

"Rifle? May I quote you in this summation? Or use the recording?"

Ochin glanced sharply downward, but Cheladin was without a trace of humor on her face.

"If the Ambassador permits. My thoughts are merely those of a Rifle ..."

Vepal nodded at Cheladin.

"You may quote my second in command, who is Ochin, Master Rifle."

If Ochin drew in a breath at being so named it was drowned in a distant rumble. Above, distant echoes, as if someone ran two or three decks overhead, and perhaps a very slight mumble of voices.

"Forward," said JinJee, which meant of up, of course, with Ochin in the lead. "Quietly!"

CHAPTER NINE

Inago was a well-run station, smelling far less of plastics and paints than most; nonetheless as they climbed the stairs there was a slightly pungent odor. Ochin in the lead was first to see its source, which was a small man working at the door of the next slide hatch, one landing up, crouching. There was at least one other there, hand in sleeve all that showed.

Ochin held back and Cheladin was beside him, taking in the same sight. She nodded and ghosted downward.

Ochin thought if he had been doing careful work on a sealed door and caught sight of a man with open blade approaching stealthily he might take pause, or take alarm. Best not to have either.

The knife then went away.

Cheladin returned, nodding and whispering ... "Make just a little noise, we go up!"

"Yes," he said in Terran, "I will."

With Cheladin a step behind, Ochin continued upward, allowing his boots to scuff a step, and then another, as she did the same. A turn of the steep stairs and by then there were five visible on the landing, several with guard hands close to holstered guns, the one working, now with an assistant, and another still in half shadow, all of them dressed in the uniforms favored by Perdition Enterprises.

"Hello," Cheladin said. "Can we all get through here, do you think? "

She and Ochin moved forward into the light, "We have two Commanders..."

Consternation, then a voice from the shadows: "Who is here?"

From below came the ambassador's firm voice:

"Vepal and Sanchez, Agent ter'Menth. Have you also been caught out on the wrong side?"

"Come ahead," said the Agent, "we believe we make progress. This station administration could use some reordering, could it not?"

#

The landing was crowded now, the walls giving back the noise of work going forth on the door as well as people too close together in a small area. Vepal recognized Recruiting Agent pen'Chouka, among those gathered, as well as ter'Menth.

Introductions included only the principals; with Cheladin as an administrative officer, the others being pointed to as Rifle, tech specialist, staff. Progress had been made, after all–the specialist had a knack and certain specialized tools permitting door access, and in the end it took that and Ochin's extra muscle to help force the thing, there being no pressure differential between the sides to speak of.

Agent ter'Menth spoke as the hatch was secured.

"Shall we find you at the Paladin's camp, Ambassador? Do you not have another staffer, your pilot? I had left a message ... for you, a reminder, at your ship but have had no reply ..."

Vepal loomed close, straight lipped.

"Another pilot on staff, Agent? Oh, the former line pilot. I had forgotten. I will need to amend my troop listing with you, for I am my own pilot now."

Agent ter'Menth's eyes went wide, but she recovered quickly.

"Do you say so? Has he been stolen away by one of the units we've signed here, then?"

"His location is of no moment, Agent. He is no longer of my unit."

Uncharacteristically, grim emotion played across her face before that expression went bland–or decisive–and the querying voice gave way to an artificially light tone.

"Well then, we may all–no, let us speak privately. The others may move forward. If we step this way for a moment ..."

The Agent bent close to the specialist, who was gathering tools, She spoke rapidly in quiet Liaden and then to the other agent, waving at them peremptorily as if shooing them on, then in Trade saying, "Walk together so that you may explain to any of the station personnel ..."

"Please, Commander Sanchez, excuse us for this moment–we shall catch up with you shortly."

JinJee looked unhappy at this, but nodded, with Cheladin staying well back.

"Commander Vepal," Ochin began stridently, but Vepal signed for silence as the Agent gave another round of rapid instruction in Liaden to her minions.

"Commander!"

Vepal turned on Ochin, then.

"Master Rifle, you have your orders. We shall be along shortly!"

Vepal and 'ter Menth both leaned somewhat in the direction of the hall when motion caught Vepal's eye.

The agent may also have seen the motion; her shoulder rose, her left arm reached, her mouth tensed as if she was going to say something, but all stopped at once as the motion was followed by the distinctive cough of three pellet gun shots, and the rustle of the agent, ear bloody and throat glistening red, falling lifeless to the floor.

By the time Vepal finished his turn two other Liadens were dead, the others thrown to the floor and held under threat of weapons.

Ochin's face was grimly pale as he spoke to Vepal in the quiet aftermath, breathy with rage.

"Sir, she'd commanded our execution and promised yours. I have protected the combined command, sir, as ordered."

Breathing was the only sound for a moment, and then the air system picked up a notch.

"We are defended, as ordered," Cheladin remarked, pulling the comm to her face. "I will report this to the station, immediately."

#

Cheladin brought tea from the dispenser for Vepal; he stood by Jin-Jee, taking comfort from her presence. They had called the station for assistance and assistance had arrived.

Ochin was under arrest. The others were witnesses or material witnesses, and possibly uncharged co-conspirators, but at the moment they were all locked in together while the stationmaster and her staff "checked the records" to decide what to do.

For Ochin, wearing the silly restraints insisted upon by the station staff, she brought a foamed double hotchoc. Ochin being seated at the table before a view screen, she sat next to him, and said, "Have you found it?"

"Exactly as I told them. Act three, scene three, <u>Of dea'Feen's Necessity</u>, by pel'Gorda."

"Show me."

He awkwardly touched the control, and–a little too loudly by the way JinJee shrank at the rapid Liaden dialog–the action continued.

Surely Cheladin knew Liaden, but the Rifle translated along with the recording, "So take them down the hall, and kill them quickly around the corner, while I take the treacherous one this way, and he will know his throat is cut."

Vepal winced, JinJee grimaced, Cheladin blew out a deep breath.

"She *said* that?"

"Yes, she was being amused, it seemed to me, to rush us all to death using a famous line from a most famous play. I could not ignore such an obvious threat! My orders ..."

"Oh, jeez!"

That was Cheladin, watching as the play continued–"Bloodthirsty bunch, were they?"

Ochin turned the sound down on the video play, finally.

"Balance was involved. Revenge, you see, revenge with malice and ..." he fought languages for a moment "... perhaps expert cunning. More than that, cunning with prideful cruelty. I've known someone like that, but he is gone."

Cheladin turned to them, JinJee and Vepal together.

"What do you think?"

JinJee shrugged, looked toward Vepal, came to the table.

"I've seen people like that myself, but this is frightening as much as enlightening. If this is an example of Balance done properly I'm not in favor of being involved with any of it."

"I would be pleased not to deal with these people," said Vepal, with sudden energy, coming to the table and nearly back-handing the screen. "Not the ones who want this."

He turned to JinJee, earnest.

"These people–Perdition and those who foment such things–they deserve enemies who are strong and who are forceful and who are ...aware that there are bounds of action. That is what The Troop was meant to insure, that cruelty would not win every time. That's why we were born and came through from the old universe to found Temp Headquarters."

Into the pause came noise from the hall outside, likely another escort to take the prisoner somewhere else. There'd been a holding cell, there'd been another holding cell, a division of the Liaden survivors from the mercs, and then there'd been a hearing in front of a tired woman with three tired confederates asking the same questions . . .

And there'd been experts who spoken to the remaining Liadens. Things had taken longer than they ought to have, what with the station dealing with a hurried exodus of dozens of ships, with the several near riots when some who'd signed the NDAs discovered that there was no kill-fee for the operation crashing without warning, that Perdition Enterprises had no more behind it than the willful conniving of a failing scheme throwing the last of their money at an operation meant to justify centuries of sabotage, intrigue, and deception.

Ochin touched the controls, freezing the screen on the image of a satisfied man sipping on tea, victorious. Two handed, Ochin raised the cup of hotchoc and sipped.

The door slid open, with a low sound of a crowd waiting outside. A woman walked in, closing the door, waving a card and wand.

She approached the only one wearing restraints.

"You're Ochin? The man who made the speech we're all hearing?"

He stood.

"That's Master Rifle Ochin, of Vepal's Small Troop?"

"Yes," he said. "Master Rifle Ochin. I understand I have been quoted."

"Yes, you have. Which one is Vepal?"

The Ambassador stood tall then, and came forward.

"You, sir, are to take charge of Master Rifle Ochin during the remainder of his visit to this station . You've got one station day to arrange . . ."

She stopped, took a crumbled sheet of hard copy from her pocket...

"Here it is. You've got one station day to arrange your necessities and get on your way. Master Rifle Ochin has the same. Stationmaster says you, Master Rifle Ochin, aren't to brandish, threaten, or be involved in any fighting. We'll deliver your weapons to ship side when you're on the way out."

"Other than that, all of you are free to go. Stationmaster and the security committee have reviewed camera and sound recordings of the incident where the deceased ordered her crew to illegally force open the door and then ordered them to kill your group, one and all–the Liaden was quite clear that this was meant to be carried out immediately, by stealth, and without provocation from your side."

The woman looked at her hard copy again, and saluted Ochin Master Rifle.

"You sir, are exonerated of any charges of murder, manslaughter, or wrongful death in this situation as you were acting in self defense as well as under orders to protect command. If the future returns you to Inago Prime you will be welcomed. Thank you for helping preserve peace on this station."

Apparently she'd run out of things to crib from hard copy notes, so she tucked the page away and smiled at the group.

"You are all free to go, if you can get past the folks waiting to thank Mr. Ochin. We'll give you a couple minutes to see if some of them will go away, or you can go out the back door, if you like."

Vepal looked to JinJee–

"One station day!"

As the messenger left they could hear the shout of honor from the waiting Paladins: "Ochin, Ochin, Ochin, Vepal, Ochin, Ochin, Ochin, Vepal!"

Ochin looked down at the restraints still wrapped around his wrists, took a deep breath, and with a sharp motion pulled them apart, leaving his arms free to move, and wristlets dangling.

"We can go now, Commander," Ochin said firmly. "I am ready."

CHAPTER TEN

They'd left through the front door, giving Master Rifle Ochin an opportunity to be celebrated by those wise enough not to blame the unmasking of a scheme with the failure of the scheme's promises to be true.

Not all of those interested in Ochin were waiting to congratulate him on his release for doing proper duty. Some, already plotters, were willing to plot again, or at least to blame.

Those people, hoodwinked as much by their failure to perform due diligence as by the deceased, were still at the bar and certain that they'd been sold out of the richest pay credits of their lives by a know-nothing newbie with too fast a gun hand.

The stationmaster pointed out there were no more accessible funds in Perdition accounts held on station. The two associated Perdition ships, locked tight as they were, were being held for inspection by a Scout and a Merc technical team still to be assembled—and thus not available to be auctioned off for any of the debt, real or imagined, that those who'd signed the NDA claimed. In other words, no recourse.

While the bars were going straight cash or backed credit only the headaches got worse as the braver—or more foolhardy—of the former Perdition allies shared what they'd agreed to, discovering over and over again that they'd contracted to accept the same thing—shares of a planetary treasury, for example, where the shares added up to multiple hundreds of percents . . . .

For his part Vepal was pleased enough to let Ochin take credit for what was, after all, the accident of their meeting ter'Menth's crew. He could but salute the purity of the Rifle's understanding of his orders.

Still, still he might need to talk to Ochin, who'd felt the need to apologize to him, twice, for shooting without warning, for–Well there, the battlefield had come upon them unbidden if not entirely unexpected, and Ochin, long away from an active front, had fallen back on his Rifle's training to take the most important target first. It had shaken Vepal, in the end, to discover his lapse and see the result, and now keeping Ochin ... he would talk to him.

Of their day's grace before leaving, the first hour was spent returning to the Paladin's bivouac, the way made more difficult by the churning in the hall of the several corps rushing for their ships before station's demand for payment and even back-payment became burdensome.

Chelly left them, her people and the station's–backed with the addition of a contingent of Paladin specialists–taking full command of the rapid dispersal of the unemployed mercs to points elsewhere. Chelly having gone in the interim from Lieutenant Cheladin to Lieutenant Commander Cheladin of Admin, she'd personally overseen the of removal Vinkleer's crew along with the implements they'd meant to use to take over the station once the expeditionary forces had gone. Altogether, ter'Menth's ambitions had been immense!

Vepal and JinJee sat side-by-side at a hasty snack thrown together to honor Ochin; the pair smiling on the troops and quaffing careful amounts of beer while reports flowed in on the progress of the station's shedding of Perdition's effects. JinJee wisely pointed out to the Master Rifle that among the mercs was a tradition of drinking a hero into such drunkenness that might not be to the best interest of Ochin's head, nor the needs of safety. Ochin, accustomed to the ambassador's gentle hand with his crew, took that suggestion seriously, carefully losing track of his beers after a sip or two so that many of the Paladins might happily recall giving the hero yet another cup.

Vepal found himself studying JinJee's face from time to time, and smiling, and found her at times smiling at him though naught had been said. She even dipped her head at one point, giving a small laugh that turned into a willful smile.

"We're too old to be smitten, you know. But damn if it doesn't feel that way to me."

Vepal nodded, pleased to know that he was not alone in feeling emotions roiling along that were far from the emotions a commander ought to be be feeling, to be filled with thoughts far from those a commander with an imminent departure ought to be to thinking.

They laughed together, raised glasses to each other, and looked out among the troops as JinJee shared a note on her comm from Chelly–

"Lyr Cats assembled for lift-out; they'll be going to Surebleak and will be carrying my report to the new merc sector headquarters there. I'll ask them to share portions with the Scouts, Ochin's report in particular, if you agree."

Vepal thought, handing the device back to JinJee.

"They will be told that they were targeted for invasion?"

He watched her face, pleased to see her expression firm with thought. She was, perhaps, a work of art, even her willingness to share her considerations with one who'd been accidentally met during a brawl.

"If they don't already know that some see them as vulnerable, don't you think they should? It isn't like they've got Clutch living on planet, is it? Best that the Scouts, and Korval, know—but Korval must know their danger!"

He gave a very short nod of assent, seeing the eyes of various of her troops surveying the pair of them. They were good soldiers, if most of them under-grown....

JinJee smiled, too—

"They admire you, you know," she said with a wry smile, "and they admire and like your Rifle. I can't think what the change of people's attitudes might be when they discover that the Yxtrang ambassador stepped into a merc problem bordering on critical mass and defused it with the application of considered force."

Vepal shook his head, barely suppressing his laugh.

"But that is not what happened, JinJee. We merely—"

"You merely acted in good faith at all points in this mess, which is more than can be said for several commanders I needn't mention. Well, one, yes, I will—Orburt Vinkleer and the Vinkleer Cooperative are still under guard by the station, and the story of your first meeting is going to be wrapped up in their trying to corner the Lyr Cat medical team and steal them for their own corps. Vinkleer may survive here— he station civilians will not want his blood specifically on their hands—but they may pass him along to the mercs. I am not sure he will survive in that case, my friend, since he will make a very thorough lesson by not living out the Standard.

"But there, no doubt about Vepal and Vepal's Small Troop. You were on the right side from the start. Cautious about ter'Menth, willing to let me take care of Vinkleer's goons without killing them outright—Chelly's telling people, and Chelly's going to end up on the committee the station's putting to together have a hearing on him. You won't be here, but my soldiers have already given evidence on that little fracas and it may well be that Vinkleer will be simply stripped of everything by the mercs. If the station doesn't space him for fomenting insurrection and endangering the integrity of the air system he may be seen more as a pawn than an actor in all of this. Course there's hardly a way to get an unbiased hearing at this point, since everyone knows he was the first to sign with Perdition and was acting as their bully squad."

Vepal listened, not only to hear her point but to hear her speak. Well, yes, the High Command had not been sending their regular and booster vaccinations, nor the money on time nor ... perhaps his hormones and commander-sense were out of kilter after all this time on detached duty. He was not prone, now, to be sorry for it and the unexpected joy of this late adventure.

"Friend of mine, what will you do?"

Vepal sighed, JinJee again having reached the same point in his thought processes as he, no matter through what means.

"The station tells me they are not charging us for our stay but they wish us to go as soon as we may, in case there is luck involved. Given that, I hesitate to discuss these happenings at length with the High Command until I have more to offer than to tell them that a spy has been decommissioned and that their proposed ally has been demonstrated as a fraud. I am too sane to believe that decision was properly routed through all the High Command. I'm afraid that Ochin's summation is apt–perhaps I should simply make him my Aide and let his Rifle go!–but there, I wish not to abandon my mission and I wish not to abandon the hope of dealing properly with the universe according to our First Orders."

JinJee nodded, leaning in, and said, "Wishes are not acts, as we both well know. I will be taking the bulk of my command to Werthing, where I own a quarter share of a small training reserve.

We will have a short break there, to refresh ourselves–space station life is not the best for keeping in shape and on target."

She paused, smiled almost shyly.

"You are welcome to set Werthing as a destination if you will. I will give you the code; do not fail to understand your welcome."

He brightened at the thought, felt himself flush with the visibility of his eagerness. It took an act of will to master his urge to say yes and turn that into a regretful shake of head.

"Perhaps I will add that to the list of future destinations, depending on our other travels and communications. First I think I will take my ship to Omenski, since I have need of refreshing myself as pilot. There is a service order of peace-seekers there; they permit ambassadors and mediators a place to stay in pursuit of peace–I have been there before and find a certain measure of a accord with them–and it is an easy Jump from there, I see, to this Surebleak."

JinJee's eyes widened.

"You'd go to Korval?"

"I am, after all, looking for point of action to offer to the High Command, an embraceable change point, since at least some of the commanders seem disinclined to continue with our recent floundering. Korval is not averse to dealing with the members of the Troop, nor with any group that offers honorable alliance. Perhaps they will know a path forward if they are not themselves the ally I need."

He smiled wanly.

"The service order I speak of at Omenski? They have a beautiful campus on a lake, a serene place where meditation is favored, and life is unhurried. My plan is to hurry there, take full consideration of my situation and that of Ochin, perhaps to study, briefly, on the possibilities before me, as well as the ways of Liaden tea, which I may need if I am to deal with this Tree and Dragon. Then, before speaking to the High Command, I *will* speak to Korval."

JinJee nodded and gave a deep nod which was nearly a bow.

"Well considered, my friend."

Someone called for her attention, then pointed.

"See this, here, JinJee, look at this!" and she held up her hand to delay that a moment, reached out and touched his arm gently.

"Your plan has merit. If your meditation shows you that you need a new path, my friend, you can come to me on Werthing, or wherever I am. We can perhaps ..."

The call for her attention grew louder, and Vepal stood as she did. The press of leave-taking upon them, he dared to take her hand in his and squeeze it tightly, and to feel the brave squeeze she gave his in return.

"Yes", he said, "perhaps we can. I would be honored to see you again."

ABOUT THIS BOOK

Once upon a time, back when the joint Lee & Miller career was in the hands of relatively new writers named Lee & Miller, we had an editor tell us that our stories had too many characters. The editor demanded that we pull out some threads of a character's story from a book, to make it leaner. Alas, having gotten close to where we were going with the initial set of characters, we saw that we weren't simply writing books, but a universe. We followed orders reluctantly, creating plotting problems for later books. Still, we thus learned to thread story lines and to dethread story lines; under threat of literary abandonment the writing went on and our stories became Liaden Universe® stories.

Thankfully, readers began to recognize Liaden stories *as* Liaden stories and so our community of readers and fans was able to grow as our own understanding of how we needed to proceed grew.

Shout of Honor is a quintessentially Liaden Universe® story, dealing in fact with the properly capitalized big three of the oft-cited themes of the series: Honor, Balance, and Necessity. Of course the fourth theme–the always popular Hint of Romance–hangs right along with them. As with Jethri from *Balance of Trade* and the characters in recent Pinbeam Books chapbooks like *Degrees of Separation* and *Fortune's Favors,* these characters have been developing around the edges of stories for awhile, waving their metaphorical hands and ideas at us, reminding us that we really should look in their direction even if saving the universe and building a new one.

It is hard for us to call the story of Vepal and JinJee *new*. While we saw the events swirling along inevitably from Clan Korval's defense of–and subsequent expulsion from– Liad, these characters were part of our understanding of the changes going on in the fabric of the interstellar communities we'd been working with. Our initial thought was to bring these characters forward by threading their stories along with the action in our novels *Neogenesis* and *Accepting the Lance.* Portions of their story developed as we plotted and considered an arc–a five book arc, we thought!–wrapping up the Department of the Interior's nefarious plans and bringing the burgeoning younger generation of Korval into the fray.

Since we write organically and listen to muses, as those five books came together the characters here *kept* telling us their story. We listened, trying to compress them into the main line of narrative, to no avail. While taking place during the same time as the novels the characters here didn't directly intersect with action taking place front and center. Still, we needed to know about them, and clearly the stories needed to be told. Also? A lot happens simultaneously in a universe.

Too many characters? Well, maybe not. We didn't want any single book to go beyond the comfortable 120,000 or 150,000 words length we and our readers knew. We didn't, also, wish to attempt that non-traditional book offering itself to us by having five, six, or seven multi-threaded color-coded and time-lined columns side by side. We wouldn't be comfortable writing it and we're sure our publisher wouldn't be comfortable trying to package such an approach.

So there you have it. We're continuing to investigate our universe and our characters in a way readers and writers can get at them. In order to keep the book and story lengths reasonable, to keep the story threads manageable, we've given *Shout of Honor* the dignity to exist independently. Thanks for reading on!

—Sharon Lee and Steve Miller
Cat Farm and Confusion Factory

May 2019

ABOUT THE AUTHORS

Maine-based writers Sharon Lee and Steve Miller teamed up in the late 1980s to bring the world the story of Kinzel, an inept wizard with a love of cats, a thirst for justice, and a staff of true power.

Since then, the husband-and-wife team have written dozens of short stories and twenty plus novels, most set in their star-spanning, nationally-bestselling, Liaden Universe®.

Before settling down to the serene and stable life of a science fiction and fantasy writer, Steve was a traveling poet, a rock-band reviewer, reporter, and editor of a string of community newspapers.

Sharon, less adventurous, has been an advertising copywriter, copy editor on night-side news at a small city newspaper, reporter, photographer, and book reviewer.

Both credit their newspaper experiences with teaching them the finer points of collaboration.

Steve and Sharon are jointly the recipients of the E. E. "Doc" Smith Memorial Award for Imaginative Fiction (the Skylark), one of the oldest awards in science fiction. In addition, their work has won the much-coveted Prism Award (*Mouse and Dragon* and *Local Custom*), as well as the Hal Clement Award for Best Young Adult Science Fiction (*Balance of Trade*), and the Year's Best Military and Adventure SF Readers' Choice Award ("Wise Child").

Sharon and Steve passionately believe that reading fiction ought to be fun, and that stories are entertainment.

Steve and Sharon maintain a web presence at: http://korval.com

NOVELS BY SHARON LEE AND STEVE MILLER

The Liaden Universe®
Fledgling
Saltation
Mouse and Dragon
Ghost Ship
Dragon Ship
Necessity's Child
Trade Secret
Dragon in Exile
Alliance of Equals
The Gathering Edge
Neogenesis
Accepting the Lance

Omnibus Editions
The Dragon Variation
The Agent Gambit
Korval's Game
The Crystal Variation

Story Collections
A Liaden Universe Constellation: Volume 1
A Liaden Universe Constellation: Volume 2

A Liaden Universe Constellation: Volume 3
A Liaden Universe Constellation: Volume 4

NOVELS BY SHARON LEE

The Carousel Trilogy
Carousel Tides
Carousel Sun
Carousel Seas

Jennifer Pierce Maine Mysteries
Barnburner
Gunshy

THANK YOU

Thank you for your support of our work.
 –Sharon Lee and Steve Miller